Defiant

USA Today Bestselling Authors

URSULA SINCLAIR
KASSANNA

Editor – Phoenix Pen

Line Editor – Refreshed Edits

Cover Model- Tyler Halligan

Photographer- Golden Czermak

AUTHORS NOTES

While this is a work of fiction, we recognize there is language and situations in this story that are offense and hurtful to many, ourselves included. But we felt it was necessary in order to tell Dachs and Harper's story. Ultimately, this is a love story of hope and shows that hate cannot survive when faced with truth and love.

Also for Bostonians, we did take liberties when describing the trains. It was necessary to drive the storyline.

1
______

HARPER

This could not be happening to me—today of all days.

"But Dad!"

"No Harper, this will be good for you. Take the subway to school. It won't kill you. We'll decide about your car when we get back next week."

I took the phone away from my ear for a second to stare at it. What was there to decide? The damn car had broken down on me. I should be arranging for a loaner until I could choose a brand new car. "Fine, I'll take an Uber or Lyft!"

"No you won't; you'll take the subway."

What was wrong with him?

"I'm not even sure where to catch it. Does it even run straight to school?"

"You know it does. There's a Harvard Station right on campus. You're a senior, a year younger than most seniors, I might add, and you're studying economics. You're smart, so figure it out. And, if you can't, then I'm sure there's an App that can help you. You'll be fine. We'll see about the car when I get home. We'll either get it fixed or get you a new one."

"Okay, okay, but I'm aiming for a new one. This is the second time I've had a problem with it in a year."

"We'll see about getting you a new car. Your mother says, hello and she can't wait to see you when we get back.'"

I disconnected the phone, not even bothering to comment. That woman was not my mother, and no matter how many times I repeated it to him it didn't stick. Teresa was actually his third wife and only ten years older than I am. I'm twenty-one. My dad's sixty.

My mother was his first wife and died ten years ago, the second one lasted all of two seconds before he divorced her. He married the housekeeper's daughter two months later, who dropped out of college to help him 'raise me'. Mind you, I can count on my hands the number of times I spent more than a week with that woman, and that includes the holidays. Yeah, she tries to be friends, and I love my dad, so I tolerate her. The only good news is Daddy loves me back, and when my mother almost died in childbirth he had a vasectomy. So, I didn't have to worry about half sibs—a fact that pisses Teresa off to this day; she didn't realize until it was too late, she couldn't have his child. Oh, she dragged him to doctors to see if it could be reversed, but no can do. So, she settled for trying to make nice with me.

I was still pissed. It was great for my father to say that I should take the subway. He's not the one who has to take the damn thing. I'm pretty sure my dad has never been on the MBTA, the Boston T, and his wife probably hasn't taken the subway since she married my dad. For a second, I thought about calling an Uber anyway. But, Dad would see it since it was on his account. And, I've always been a good daughter, doing as I was supposed to do—making all the right decisions for the future I'd planned out for myself and that he'd encouraged. But, I was no fool. If I had any hopes of getting a new car, I better do as he said.

"Hey," I said to the guy behind the counter at the service shop. "How far is the T from here? I'm trying to get to the Harvard Station."

He gave me directions. Apparently, I had to go to some station crossing and take any train that would allow me to switch over to the red line. That would drop me right on campus. Seemed easy enough. There was a T entrance about a five minute walk from the shop. Which might have accounted for the funny look he gave me when I asked for directions.

I tightened up my Balenciaga backpack and set out. I was just glad I had on comfortable shoes because I only had three classes today; two of them were in the same building, but the third was a hike.

I joined the flow of masses on the sidewalk, moving in the direction I needed to go. Everyone seemed to be heading for the T. I would have thought rush hour would be over by now but guess not. Hopefully, all of these people weren't getting on the same train I was. That would suck.

I waited in line to buy a card to ride the thing. Thank God the machines took credit cards, otherwise that would have been a problem. I never carried cash. Then, it still took me a few minutes to figure the damn thing out. Three people had already come and gone, getting their cards in the line next to me before I got mine, and only because the lady behind me pointed out the right button I needed to press. You'd think it would be a simple process. Like 1, 2, 3 just follow these steps. But noooo, wasn't that simple.

Can't say I was really liking the metallic scent of the trains before I even saw them or the feel of the concrete surrounding me underground. At least the map I checked showed me where to go, and I wasn't standing shoulder to shoulder with people, like over on the other platform. The lights embedded in the floor began flashing a few minutes after I arrived. Thank you, God, I didn't have long to wait.

By the time I made my way on board, after getting shoved a time or two by people exiting, I took the first seat I found near the window facing another row of seats, already occupied by one other person, but he had the aisle seat. I didn't really glance at him, but I could feel his eyes on me. I quickly took off my backpack and placed it on the seat next to me, hoping no one would sit there and crowd me. I also kept one hand on the strap, just in case anyone got any ideas. I settled back, but these seats were damned uncomfortable, at least the one directly across from me was empty. I could stretch my legs a bit. It was then I got around to glancing at the guy seated in the aisle.

Shit on a stick, he was gorgeous. If I'd known guys that looked like him rode public transportation, I'd have been using it for years. Then again, probably not. But damn, he was fine.

I pulled my phone out and raised it, like I was trying to read something. I was really trying to snag a picture of him. I pushed the button just as he moved his head a fraction in my direction, and his gaze met mine. I quickly glanced down.

Caught.

Damn. I had a boyfriend. I couldn't flirt with this guy. And, as good looking as he was, I could tell by his clothes and the tats I could see on most of the exposed areas of his skin, he wasn't my type. I texted the picture of him to my best friend Serena anyway. She too appreciated good eye candy. Her reply came back fast.

'HOLY SHIT!!!'
'I know right!'
'Get his number.'
'I don't think so.'
'Gotta run. Get his damn number or give him mine.'
'LOL'

I turned and tried to look out the window but there was nothing to see. Then I noticed I could see his reflection on the glass. Damn, was that the initials HH on his neck? Mine were HH, Harper Hodges. Was that some kind of sign?

Shit, he was staring at me. I would have chuckled, but I had to play it cool. Should I say something to him? No. He's the dude, he should approach me first, not the other way around. I don't have to throw myself at anyone. *Ever.* Not about to start now. But damn, he was fine. I kept thinking that, but it was the truth.

I shifted and adjusted my backpack for something to do as the train came to a stop. I glanced up and our gazes met, again. Crap, we were doing some serious eye fucks. I noted he took out his phone. I wondered if he was trying to sneak a pic of me. I smiled. I put his picture in Google images and did a search to see if I could find him on social media. A few hundred pictures came up, and while some of the guys resembled him, I really didn't find him on there. Too bad. Then again, maybe that's a good thing. I might have been tempted to send him a friend request—tell him I was the girl on the train. Yeah, like he didn't meet a lot of girls on the train.

The train had stopped a few times before I glanced up again, finally realizing my stop was the next one. Well damn it anyway. That was not enough time to get him to say something to me. I wondered if he rode the T all the time. It might be worth my while to ride it again tomorrow.

As the train pulled into the school station I stood and grabbed my bag. His long legs took up the space between the seats, but I didn't bother to even say anything to him. I stepped right over them like they weren't even there and moved past him toward the door. But, when the train stopped, I glanced quickly in his direction only to see him staring back at me.

Yeah, even though the train ride wasn't anywhere near as

smooth as the shocks on my car, and the smell of way too many humans in a confined space left much to be desired, I would be on the train again tomorrow. If only to see if I could find him again. Besides, I knew what to expect now, and I'd bought a damn card for a week. I couldn't figure out how to just buy one for a day. So, might as well not waste it. I got off and began walking toward my exit as the train left the station. I could see him sitting in his seat. Our eyes locked for the last time and neither of us looked away until the train moved out of sight.

2

DACHS

The deep, muffled rumble of the train along with the smooth rocking motion was soothing. It was rare I had time alone to think. If it wasn't my family demanding I devote time to our pierogi shop, that I hate, then it was meeting up with members of the brotherhood, which I love. It's not hard to see where I stand. I don't hide my beliefs, and if necessary, I will back them up. A first generation German American born to immigrant parents, I am a true Aryan.

Early morning class at tech school is brutal, but connections will only get a person so far without an education. My buddy got me a spot at an electrical company as an apprentice journeyman. It is hell, listening to those lazy ass ethnics I work with whine about how unfair their lives are. They cry about money but only got the job because they fit a certain racial profile, unfair to those of us in the true white race.

Fucking niggers.

Today, at least I would get a break since it was my day off.

I straightened out my legs and rested my head on the back of the seat. Surrounded by empty seats, it was good. No need to hold my tongue, and every time someone passed and hesitated, eyeing the open spaces beside me, I'd simply flex my fingers or roll my head on my neck. The tattoos I sported spoke volumes. My cell vibrated in my pocket. A long sigh escaped past my lips as I dug the phone out. My peace didn't last long.

"Yeah."

"I sent you the location for tonight's meeting," Bruno muttered. A Jersey boy transplant, my friend and second in command of our burgeoning group, skipped his hometown after a jump-in went bad—blood in and blood out, turned out the guy being initiated was an informant. Mother fucker got a lesson he would never forget.

That was all I needed to know. "Same time?" I smiled at a perky blonde as she bounced by. Now, that was more like it—baby blue irises, platinum curls and a tight ass. I sat up and watched her as she sauntered down the aisle. There was nothing prettier than a pure blooded woman.

"Seven."

"I'll be there." I ended the call, settled back, and hunkered down into my seat, closing my eyes. The stop/start motion made me sluggish. My lids drifted shut, just for a minute, and the blare of a horn jolted me awake. I opened my eyes to find her peering at me—a black girl. God, of all the people who could have shared space with me, it was a monkey. I watched her; even animals could be cute. Didn't she see the annoyance on my face?

Her hair was long and nappy. She couldn't even bother to comb the snags from her strands. Her skin was the color of heavily creamed coffee, and her shape...I narrowed my eyes. It was hard to tell with her seated. She was no longer looking directly at me, instead tinkering with her phone. An unusual aroma reached my nose. Sweet and flowery, it wafted from her direction, combined with the train stench the smell came off more like sweet smelling shit. Why the hell did she keep peeking at me from under her long ass lashes? Things like her were a dime a dozen. I still cannot understand the fascination that some guys have with women of other races. Mixing should never-ever happen, it just dilutes the blood.

Now, she was openly staring, hiding behind the little device in front of her face. It wouldn't take much for me to just lean forward and snatch that cell from her hands. Clamping down the urge to lash out, I swallowed my annoyance. Too many people. If I assault her now, there will be witnesses. What was the debate? I could ease over to sit beside her and slam a few punches into her belly for the blatant disrespect... Hurting an untainted white woman was a big hell no in my book, but Blackies, they have no value. Hmm—maybe socially, thanks to the damn liberals that are trying to control the country. I glanced around. A crowd can also work in my favor. It would be nothing to teach her a lesson and slip away. Not enough people filled the train.

The car slid to a stop, and she stood. Without a word she stepped over my legs. I resisted the urge to grab her wrist. In my presence, she needed to acknowledge me—respect her superiors. I scooted forward, her fingers within my grasp. Some asshole in a hurry jostled my arm. She kept moving. I made a fist, slamming back into my seat. Through the glass I caught a glimpse of her looking back. Laughter burst past my lips. The foolish little negro girl had no idea how much danger she'd just courted. I held her gaze as the train moved on.

The devil you know.

The phrase popped through my mind. I was the demon she didn't know. A snort escaped past my lips. Would she watch me like that if she knew the things I could do to her? Some brown skin moved past me, leaving in their wake the stench of ripe sweat and rank body odor. Tears brimmed my eyes, and I stood to escape the smell lingering at waist level. The next stop, I got off. Fresh air would go a long way toward clearing my sinuses.

Trotting up the stairs two at a time, I exited the short tunnel into bright afternoon sunlight. It would be a while before I was needed for anything.

I pulled the cell free and tapped in a number. Rings abruptly stopped, giving way to silence.

"I know you're there."

"You only call me when you want something." Becky's soft tone flowed into the earpiece.

"I'm not far from your place." I can get my dick wet and still make the meeting.

"I'm busy."

"So, am I, but don't I always make time for you?" Becky was a block over. I could be at her front door in ten minutes. "You make all my stresses disappear."

"A booty call? Is that all I am to you?"

Yeah. Becky belonged to the Brotherhood. Her pussy could be claimed by any one of us. "No, you are the one woman in my life that understands me."

Lying was a way of life for me. To my parents, to my brothers, to this girl, to ease their minds or keep them in the dark. Whatever was safest for me.

This was a new age. Thanks to social media there was an awareness, and right or wrong was decided by the masses. For people like me the internet was not my friend. One wrong move, and my face would spread across the web and my family's business would suffer. My brothers would be marked as racist. That was a really broad term. It's not like we didn't like the colored people, it was just better if they didn't occupy U.S. soil. The damn animals came from somewhere, and I would happily send them back to their lands of origin.

"The key is where it always is." Becky's voice broke through my thoughts.

I ended the call, passing a bucket filled with limp roses

outside of a convenience store. I hesitated and kept moving. Becky and I didn't have that kind of relationship. She was a good fit and a proud sister to the brotherhood, meant to propagate the white race. Becky truly believed in the cause and supported it. I could take her out for a burger another day. I hiked faster, the idea of sinking into her undiluted sweetness giving me the energy boost I needed, anticipation sending jolts of awareness to my crotch. I turned down the sidewalk of her street—I thought of her deep blue eyes holding mine as I thrust into her. Slowly, those pretty irises morphed into light brown ones surrounded by dark, long, thick lashes. I shook my head.

What the hell?

Why was a nigger invading my thoughts?

I trotted up the stoop steps and into the converted apartment building, stopping at Becky's door. I flipped over the corner of the mat and retrieved the key, straightening to slide it in the lock. I opened the door to a cool, shadowed interior. I knew my way around the place, moving straight for the bedroom.

Becky knew what I wanted and was already naked and in bed. "You got here fast."

I needed to erase the image of the Blackie stuck in my memory. I lunged for Becky, wrapping my fingers around her ankle and dragging her to the edge of the mattress. "I'm a little annoyed."

She spread her thighs. "I'll take care of you." A smirk lifted one side of her mouth.

I unzipped my jeans and yanked them and my underwear down. Kicking them off, I dropped down on to the bed and stroked my dick. "Suck me off." Seeing Becky's pretty blonde strands brushing my skin as she gave me head should be enough to make me forget.

3
____

HARPER

"Hey baby, see you later tonight?"

The arms wrapping around my waist as I walked out of the lecture hall, and the sound of his voice were very familiar. He caught me unaware because all through class, I kept glancing at my phone and the picture I'd snuck of the man on the train. Still wondering about it.

Him.

This wasn't really like me to be so obsessive over cute guys—shoes yes, guys no, especially since I had one of my own.

I turned into Justin's embrace and smiled. His hazel eyes, cut features and olive complexion, highlighting his Greek heritage, still turned me on as it did from the first time I'd met him a year ago when I interned for the brokerage firm where he worked. At twenty-six, he was a few years older than I. As a favor to me, he'd agreed to be a guest lecturer for another class down the hall. I should have remembered he was going to be here today and called him for a lift to class. But the morning had been hectic dealing with my car and my first T ride.

"Hey, you with me?" Justin asked.

The slight squeeze at my waist had me refocusing on Justin. "Yeah, just thinking about the class. How was your lecture?"

"Great. It was a lot of fun being on the other side of a lecture hall for a change. And, my boss loved me being a guest lecturer. I even got invited back. I might be able to turn this into a regular thing."

"That's great." Justin was all about upward mobility, and he was fast rising in his firm. "Keep this up and you'll be a director soon."

"For sure."

Especially since he started handling some of my dad's accounts a few months ago, growing his portfolio. If Justin kept it up he could make it happen by the end of the year.

"So, will I see you later tonight?" he asked.

"Sure, sounds good. But, you're going to have to pick me up."

"No problem. I'd say let's grab a bite now, but I have a meeting to get to in Quincy and with traffic, I'll already be a bit late."

"Shoot, I was going to ask you to give me a ride home."

"Why? Where's your car?"

"In the shop. They have to order some part for it. I got a text, it won't be ready for another day or two." All the more reason why it was just time to get me a new car, I had no time to deal with cars breaking down. I'll be having a chat with my father when he gets back from his vacation.

"Damn, sorry babe. But, I can give you a ride to class tomorrow."

He pulled me up against his body. I could feel the hardness of his thighs, and I grinned. He worked out almost every day during the week, and it showed.

"I don't mind, especially since we can have breakfast first," he said then kissed the side of my ear.

"Thanks, but I'm good. I won't need a ride. I'll Uber or something. I know it's out of your way."

"You sure?"

I nodded. Not exactly sure why I was turning down his ride, in a comfy, cushy car for smelly bumpy public transportation. But it had something to do with a set of ice blue eyes and tats.

We both turned to walk out of the building, but he held my hand. "How'd you get to school this morning, anyway?"

"The T."

He chuckled. "You on the T? That must have been culture shock."

I wasn't sure why I was irked by his laughter and statement, even though I'd felt the same way when I spoke to my dad, and he told me to take the train, like it was a joke. "I'm not like that!" I protested, even knowing it to be true. In my twenty-one years, I'd never even taken a public school bus. The private school I went to until I graduated high school had its own fleet of private blue buses with great shocks, soft leather seats and air conditioning. And, I only took those for field trips.

Justin just laughed some more at my denial and kissed me quickly. "I'll see you tonight. Seven."

I stood there for a moment watching him saunter away, unable to stop myself from comparing him to someone else. Both men seemed tall, but wore similar builds very differently. Justin was sharp, urbane. His silk suit cost more than most people's rent and his shoes were made of the finest Italian leather. His car was the latest BMW model. His firm leased them for him, and they turned them over at the end of a year, only to get a newer one. I don't know why he was laughing at me? Wasn't like he ever took the T either.

Still, Justin fit in my world and me in his. Whereas the man on the subway seemed anything but civilized. He appeared rough around the edges; there was a hardness to him, and it wasn't just the ink I could see on his hands and neck. He didn't quite fit in my higher educated, high socio economic universe. His bank account shouldn't matter, even if it did, but I sensed more to him underneath it all.

Weird.

I pulled out my phone to call an Uber, but instead, pulled up the picture again. I stared at those eyes. Cold, pale blue eyes stared back at me. But, there were shadows buried deep within them. I didn't know him well enough to even try to determine what his thoughts were. But I wanted to.

"Who are you? Why should I even care?" I spoke the words in a whisper.

What I think I see is probably just a trick of the light in the shot. Yet, I pocketed my phone and found myself heading toward the T station.

Unfortunately, the trains were very crowded. All those college students from campus heading home or to jobs. I wasn't able to get a seat this time and forgot about trying to see if he was on the train—too many bodies. I'm only five-four so I had to hang onto a pole to stay upright. Then others kept pressing around me trying to do the same thing. At least with every lurching motion, I didn't have to worry about falling because those same bodies kept me upright.

Oh my God! Would this hellish ride ever come to an end? It came time for me to get off and transfer; thank God it wasn't too long of a ride. I decided I'd Uber the rest of the way home. I got out of the station and did that. But, I found myself scanning the platform, the train as it went by, even the street for a specific tattooed figure.

I'd just settled back in the Uber when I got a text.

'Well did you talk to him?'

I rolled my eyes after reading Serena's text.

'No, of course not. I have a boyfriend. Remember?'

'Boring. Besides, there's no ring on your finger.'
'I'm still in a relationship.'
Yet why did I keep thinking about another guy?
'Where were you anyway?'
'My car's in the shop. Can you believe, I had to take the subway.'
'Good for you! How was it?'
'Well, you saw the view.'
'Nice view. You taking the T again tomorrow?'
'Yeah, car's going to be in the shop for a couple of days.'
'Oh, say hello to Mr. Brooding and Sexy for me.'

I got home to my condo and headed straight for my shower. My clothes took on the accumulation of everyone else's day sweat. I need to get it off me first and then work on my research paper. I had a one bedroom condo with a den or study; it's where my desk and text books were. After my shower, I changed to yoga pants and a tank, then got down to work on my paper. I wanted to complete it tomorrow. I'd finish it tonight, but I had a date with Justin in a couple of hours.

I got a good chunk of my work done and sat back, glancing around my place. It was in one of the newer buildings and Daddy paid a mint for it. But, it was also an investment. It was all my idea; I found the place. I used to drive past the construction site on my way to Serena's. I did some checking and presented him with the idea and stats of the neighborhood and projections for what else was going in there. Daddy was more than happy to scoop the condo up. I'd had it for a year now, and it was already worth twenty thousand dollars more than what we paid for it. Daddy made me cough up some of the funds too. I loved my condo; it was all in my name, and I decorated it myself. A far cry, I was sure from most college grads or undergrads, the floors were all wide planked dark gray wood. The kitchen, which I didn't use very often, was all shades of gray and white with state of the art appliances. The living room and bedroom carried the same shading of light gray, but where as the living room had more color to it with cobalt blues and browns, my bedroom was a soft lilac.

The only room that looked like a student lived there was the den with all the textbooks. But my place suited me. I wondered what kind of place tattoo guy lived in? I really need to stop that.

As I stood in front of the mirror, putting on the two carat diamond earrings I'd gotten for my eighteenth birthday and the matching five carat tennis bracelet, I realized I wasn't all that excited about this date. I knew Justin and I would go to one of his favorite restaurants and have a great dinner. He had fabulous taste, always aware of the latest trendiest places. We'd talk about his job and the firms that have been courting me for an internship that would lead to a job offer. Then we'd come home, mine or his; since I had class tomorrow, probably mine, and fuck. We did that two nights ago, and we'll do it again tonight, and I was sure again over the weekend. Maybe even get out of the city to some quaint bed and breakfast in upstate New York or even the Hamptons. It had become routine. Most people would give a toe for this life, yet, I was—unsettled.

My doorbell rang. I forced a smile on my face. "Get over yourself," I told my reflection and went to answer the door.

4

DACHS

She was there. Sandwiched between T riders, the look on her face, the disgust. Who was she to have any feelings at all? The simple fact that she could roam free without restriction angered me. If you aren't pure blooded you should be kept to your own area with your people. It wasn't my first time seeing niggers on the T. I cocked my head to the side to stare at her. She wasn't any different than the other things that disgraced the city, still *her* presence rankled.

Slowly, I worked my way closer. Anger roiled in my belly. Not just for her being there but for the men, only the men surrounding her. The train lurched to a stop, and I had to grab the pole to keep from falling into the person beside me. The older white lady put her hand up to keep me in place. I smiled down at the woman with varying shades of gray hair twisted up into a bun.

She smiled and the kindness in it reached her eyes. I pushed back against the masses bearing down on me to give her room. She patted my bicep and mouthed the words *thank you* as she squeezed past me and through the open doors. On the platform I spied *that* girl. She'd exited the car and looked lost. I took a step forward and caught myself as the doors slid shut. What the hell was I thinking? She was a nigger, that couldn't be denied, even given her bright skin tone. If she was any lighter she could pass for white. Not good, an unsuspecting man could end up with tainted children. She was a walking, breathing, lie. Yet, in that moment, I thought of her as human. No, before that, when she was surrounded by *all* the male commuters. Seems her attraction was universal. Didn't the bible talk about shit like this. What was her name? She brought down biblical icons. Bathsheba, another black bitch breaking down a race of exceptional men. For a moment, I fell into that trap and was willing to stand behind her and keep the men at bay. I pressed my lips together.

However, she got around, whatever was going on with her was not my problem. I shouldn't have any feelings one way or another about that black thing. Focus on my brothers, only my brethren. Find another woman, maybe someone other than Becky, a woman fresh to the cause. That would set me straight again. A female that held onto my beliefs and supported our movement. That might take some time. The image of that niggeress popped into my mind. I resisted the urge to slam my head into the steel pole to get her out of my head.

What the fuck?

For the time being, it was best if I buried myself in the brotherhood and helped the cause, find a way to further promote Prof's ideology. My thoughts kept repeating in my mind. *She,* that black girl, didn't belong on the train. That was obvious, just from the looks of her. Maybe I should help her go back to where she came from? I snorted. Long and loud. Riders around me glanced up. Why the hell did my mind keep going back to some black bitch?

A few stops ahead of mine, I dug out my cell and stabbed the keypad, taking my aggravation out on the device. Bruno didn't pick up, but intermittent beeps interrupted the call. I tapped the top of the screen.

"The shop is busy." My mom, Alivia, didn't bother with greetings.

Nothing new, our relationship had become strained over the years because of our different views on how we see the world. We acted more like combatants toward each other than mother and son. Mom embraced everyone, white, black, yellow or red, and good or bad she gave anyone she came across the same chance. If they needed a meal she fed them. If they needed a few bucks, she would pull some from her apron pocket. Alivia was part of the problem. Still, she was my mother. When I was small and troubled, she often dug a cotton handkerchief from that same apron to wipe my tears. Even now, when we couldn't find any common ground, if I closed my eyes I could still smell the fresh doughy scent that always seemed to surround her. I just had to make her see reason.

"So am I." I understood where this was going, but I had plans, and they didn't include returning to the pierogi shop my parents owned.

"You need to come back. Now." Alivia's voice was strained, her accent thickened.

"I'm meeting—friends. I won't be back tonight." I could try and talk some sense into her and Dad another day.

"Son."

The soft way she uttered our connection made me bristle. Had my mother cared more, she would have respected my feelings. I didn't bother to hide how I felt about other races. If she saw things my way our lives would be so much better.

"Mother," I countered, with all the indifference I felt coming across in my tone.

"Come home." They lived above the shop in a stuffy two bedroom apartment.

"I have things to do." I did. Nothing like causing a little mayhem late at night. Someone should pay for the little monkey invading my thoughts.

"If you learn how to run the business, you'll have a trade. Something to rely on if—"

"How many times do I have to tell you I don't want the fucking place?" I yelled. I sucked in a deep breath and exhaled.

More curious glances were cast my way, people averting their eyes and ducking their heads when I met their gaze. They eased away, giving me space, not that they could go far on the crowded train. I reeled in my temper. Regardless of our differences, I had never doubted her love for me. Beeps interrupted the line again.

"We'll talk later." I ended the call with Alivia. In my mind, she was my mother, and she wasn't. Although she gave birth to me, eventually I would have to break ties with her. Living with my parents wasn't comfortable. It was cheap, but I could always couch surf at a couple of brother's places until I worked out a way to get my own apartment. It was becoming clear my mother wouldn't change—which meant my dad wouldn't either. To avoid the pain of trying to make them see my view, it was better not to have a connection with them at all.

I skimmed my finger across the screen. "Yeah."

"I got a case of beer to split with ya and two bats with our names on it. There is a jump in tonight, and our esteemed leader will be making an appearance. He asked for you." Bruno chuckled.

"You had me at 'jump in.'" My evening was getting better. "I'm a couple stops away. I was coming to your house anyway." Blood in and Blood out. To be a brother meant shedding blood for the cause. Pain inflicted by the men that would serve beside you. A once in a lifetime opportunity to belong to a family that truly understood you. It also meant that if someone ever wanted to break those ties, blood would be shed to be free, and that meant giving up your life.

"Becky is bringing a few of her friends to the party."

"Oh yeah?" New pussy in a fresh batch of women who believed in our cause. I might get lucky after all.

"The girls have their own recruits to welcome."

"Sounds better and better."

"White power," Bruno screamed through the earpiece.

"White power," I yelled back and laughed, pure joy coursing through my veins.

Dirty looks were cast my way. The cab screeched and lurched as it came to another stop. I smiled as I pressed through the throng of people. Once upon a time, I couldn't be open about my preferences, but this was a new day, and the freedom to despise those that were not like me was amazingly liberating. I shoved my way to the doors, slamming my body through those things below me, daring to take a breath in my space.

I could walk the couple of blocks to Bruno's house. It would take fifteen, twenty minutes max to get there. From there, the night was young, and a jump in didn't have to happen right away. Maybe we could find some wetbacks, or niggers—nope— race robbing Jews would be better. They were the reason all the fucking sub-races believed they were even in the same league as the pure, white nation. Those damn Jews always needed a good ass whooping as a reminder. What they did to Jesus was plain wrong. What they kept doing by promoting them damn sub- humans, those fucking bastards deserved everything they got, and tonight, I would make someone feel every inch of my misery. Perhaps, if I'm lucky, several monkeys and their fucking trainers will feel the end of my bat. It's not like it would be the first time. A burst of laughter erupted past my lips as I squeezed through the doors as they shut.

Tonight, would be a good night and life is good.

5
___

HARPER

Someone shoved past me. I'd turn around to tell them something, but it wasn't the first time, and I'd learned to save my breath. By the time I'd get the first word out they'd be long gone.

My car had been fixed. I'd picked it up, but it had been sitting in my leased parking garage for a week now. No one, if they knew, would believe I'd been riding public transportation for the last week, all so I could try to talk to some guy. I'm an idiot or a romantic—same difference at this point. Serena might be the only one who would understand, if she knew.

But, there had just been something compelling about the guy on the train. It wasn't just his looks. He was no pampered pretty boy. Oh, he was panty dropping worthy alright, but more, 'I'll rip them off you rather than let you step out of them' kind of guy. I knew he'd be nothing like the young men I knew. He damn well better be worth the discomfort of public transportation. Some people apparently never heard of something called deodorant and others thought they could substitute cologne for bath water. My nose wanted to go on strike.

What the hell am I doing?

I'd asked myself that question every day as I stood on the platform waiting for the blasted train. Clearly, I didn't belong amongst the masses, not with a brand new Louis Vuitton backpack, bought directly from the store and not on some sidewalk. I stood out, and I knew it. My clothes weren't the discounted designer brands of two seasons ago or even last season. If it was on the runways last week, I was wearing it the next. I had a professional stylist at a few stores who set things aside and called me as soon as the latest fashions came in. Although I was a college student, I still dressed like the privileged one I am.

Maybe I was just bored, but I wasn't, not really. My life was good. Except maybe for my father's wife. He however, refused to get me a new car, and I'm pretty sure *she* had something to do with that decision. I planned on asking her the next time I saw her and to tell her to please stay out of my business. Still, I was doing what I wanted. I was working on a degree that would be a lucrative one, and had a paid internship lined up which would turn into a permanent position. A handsome boyfriend who was just as driven as I was, and he was great in bed. Yet, here I was on this damn train again searching for someone I didn't know but wanted to.

Pathetic.

Every day I'd been on the train it had been crowded. Was it always like this? Unless he was right next to me, I wouldn't have seen him. Although, I thought I caught a glimpse of someone with tats on their knuckles holding onto the handle from the ceiling. My stop came, and I made my way through the throng to get off. It wasn't until I stood on the platform that I caught a glimpse of him moving amongst the passengers. I stood still for a moment to see if he would get off, but the door closed and the train moved on. He'd just been taking a seat.

The passing train whipped up the wind and the cold dove into my bones. The days would only get colder. I zipped my fur lined jacket up. It was Friday, and I was meeting Serena and some friends tonight for drinks. I'd have fun with my boyfriend and friends this weekend and get rid of this weird obsession I had over a guy I never met—and never will. It's not meant to be. Come Monday, I'll get my ass back in my car. I was done. I turned and headed toward my first class.

It took me a minute to realize the buzzing to my right came from my phone. Without opening my eyes I reached for it on my nightstand. "Why?" I asked. Not ready to get up yet.

"Wakie Wakie."

"Serena. What do you want?" My voice came out dry.

"Come on, Harper. We're going to breakfast. I promise you'll love this place. Steve took me there for perogies last week, and they are the best."

"What time is it?" I moved the phone from my ear, so I could see the screen, and the time. Unfortunately, I had to open my eyes to check. I knew once I did that, there'd be no going back to sleep. It was ten in the morning. Justin and I had been out all night with Serena and some of our friends. By the time we got back to my place it was three in the morning.

"I'll be there in twenty minutes to pick you up. Is Justin still there? He can come too."

Serena disconnected. Sometimes there was no saying, 'no' to that woman. I glanced at the phone. I had half a mind to call her back and tell her 'no,' when I felt the press of Justin's lips on my back. When I stretched to put the phone down, it also moved me slightly out of his reach.

"What's up?" he asked in a groggy voice. "Was that Serena?"

"Yeah, she'll be here in fifteen minutes to pick us up."

He placed his hand on my stomach, and I flinched. He

hadn't spent the night for a week, so this was the first time we'd been alone together in a while. Normally, I'd be under him or on top by now, but I hesitated and sat up, suddenly ready to get out of bed.

"You know she'll be here soon and banging on the door to be let in, if I don't come out. I need to get up and jump in the shower."

He flopped back down on the bed. "Damn it."

I could see the tent his dick had created with the sheets and smiled as I turned my back to him and went into the shower. Surprisingly, I wasn't naked. I had managed to put on some boy shorts and a cami, but I knew he wore nothing but skin under the sheets. We'd stripped off clothing, just crawled into bed and passed out.

I brushed my teeth then jumped in the shower; a bit surprised Justin wasn't right behind me. I was almost done when I heard him enter the separated stall part of the bathroom and use it. After he stepped out and went over to the sink to brush his teeth, I called out, "I'm almost done." In case he was planning on coming in.

He opened the bathroom door just as I shut off the faucet. He held a towel out to me. "Thanks," I said and wrapped it around me as he reached past me to turn the water back on. "Are you coming with us?"

"Nah. I've got some work to catch up on. I'll go home and work for a few hours, then come back later tonight, or you can come over." He leaned forward and gave me a kiss. For a moment I pressed into him, then moved out of his arms.

It was all very nice. Time to get my head back on track.

I'd just finished getting dressed when my phone buzzed. Serena was downstairs.

Justin came out of the bathroom with a towel wrapped

around him. "You sure you want to go?" he asked, a cocky smile lighting up his face.

Damn, he looked fine. He had that whole packed and cut thing going for him, courtesy of a gluten free diet and a personal trainer. I kissed him quickly. "Later. Text me when you leave, and I'll lock the door." My condo had one of those digital key locks. I could lock and unlock it with my phone. So, I never needed to give anyone a key to get in. I also had a key for it just in case something happened to the technology, but it was a good reason not to give anyone a key to my place—certainly, not my boyfriend. Although, I did have a key to his place. He'd given it to me a couple of months ago when he needed me to pick up something for him that he'd left at home. When I'd tried to return it he'd told me to keep it. But, I never reciprocated by giving him an access code to my apartment. He'd text me, and I'd either lock or unlock the door. It worked for me, and I guess him, too.

Serena's blue Taurus was pulled right in front of the entrance. Steven was in the front passenger seat, but when he saw it was just me, he hopped into the back seat.

"I guess Justin isn't joining us?" Serena asked.

"Yeah, he's got some work to do."

"Yeah, sure," Serena replied.

"Really, I'm sure he does."

"Or, he just doesn't like us. I see the way he rolls his eyes at me," she said.

"That's not true," I countered defensively.

"Yeah, it is," Steven stated. "You know whenever we're all together, he always keeps to himself. He's there but not really there. He always sits at the edges of the group, and he likes to take you with him and monopolize your time. Like last night, he sat at the end of the bar, with you next to him. After saying 'hi' to the rest of us, I'm not sure he said another word, other than to order another drink."

Serena was nodding her head in agreement with what Steven said.

"He was just tired. I thought you all liked him."

"We do. He's a nice enough guy, but I'm not sure he likes us," Serena replied. "My family doesn't have the right connections, and Steven and Ron are gay, and he never seems to get along with any of my boyfriends."

I'd been dating Justin now for almost a year. This wasn't the first time I'd heard something similar from my friends. I know the first time he met Steven, he'd stiffened. Steven is downright beautiful, actually. If he wasn't a corporate lawyer, he'd make a fortune as a model. He's also gay. At first, I thought Justin was threatened by Steven's looks, but soon realized, it was because he wasn't comfortable being around him. But, I figured he'd just have to get over it because Steven was one of my best friends.

"Well, I like you, and that's all that matters," I said.

We pulled up in a neighborhood I didn't recognize, but the street was lined with ethnic themed restaurants. We parked a few doors down from the place where Serena said she wanted to go. As soon as I got out of the car, I froze. The sun highlighted a familiar looking short blond head of hair.

Walking out of the very place we were headed was the guy from the train. He crossed the street without looking in our direction and headed away from us. Did he live around here? I almost called out to him to wait, but what the hell would I have said if he turned around? Besides, I didn't even know his name.

"You okay?" Serena asked as she came around the car.

"Yeah, yeah." Come Monday I was getting back on the train.

6

DACHS

Was she following me?

Unexpectedly, *she'd* showed up at my parents' shop. After another fight with Alivia I was rushing out to meet my crew. The black girl and her friends were walking down the sidewalk from the opposite direction. I would have missed her if she hadn't stepped forward, and the movement caught my attention.

Just another chance encounter?

But, seeing her that day almost felt like more than that. We couldn't be friends; her skin, her very background prevented that from ever happening, so we must be destined to be enemies. I'd continued on with my day without another thought about her.

She was on the train again. I watched her peeking at me. She was close enough to reach out and touch. I tightened my hold on the handle in a white-knuckled grip. To slide my fingers across her skin would be an acknowledgment that I knew she was looking for me—the clothes, her haughty expression, her disdain. She wasn't the type to ride the T. Honestly, I couldn't see her on any form of public transportation. I rolled my shoulders to ease the tension building up between them. No niggeress, any ethnic really, should ever be in a position that allowed them to be better off than their superior counterparts. It gave them a privilege complex they shouldn't have.

A couple of times could be a coincidence, but I had seen her more than a few times, and our gazes had met on occasion. She'd get off at the Harvard University stop; she was probably a fucking student there. Probably got in on some kind of program for poor blacks. She dressed well enough; her clothes could be designer, but those shirts and shit were easy enough to get from a consignment shop. Didn't mean she was smart, just savvy and entitled. I cocked my head, staring at her but not really seeing her. Instead, the instances of our run ins played through my mind like a movie.

She kept staring at me, hiding behind her phone, trying to get pics of me. I knew what she was doing, and her nerve plucked at mine. The more I see her though, I can't quite work up the same anger. It was more of a curiosity. I wouldn't exactly call her pretty, but I could see how an uneducated white man might look twice. I shook my head. What the hell was I thinking? She was the worst kind of black, one that thought they should have the same liberties as their white counterparts. These motherfuckers took our jobs and status. They trampled on our pride and cried foul whenever we raised our voices to denounce it—like *we* are wrong. The train jerked, and I shifted to the side. She moved too, slipping past the people between us. I reached out to steady her and pulled my hand back just as quickly as I thrust it out. Up close, I realized her hair wasn't black, more of a deep sable brown. For the briefest moment we locked gazes. Surprise was evident in her expression. Wide eyes, lips that formed a perfect 'O'. Just like that first day. Although we weren't nearly as close.

On the train, I turned away, ignoring her. Jumbled words

through a scratchy speaker fell down around us. My stop was next. I pushed my way through the crowd to the sliding doors. My neck warmed as if I was being watched, and I glanced over my shoulder to check and see if she was staring at me. She wasn't there. A sense of relief—no it wasn't that. It was something I couldn't quite put a name to, washed through me. I felt like I could breathe when I hadn't realized I was actually holding my breath.

The train ground to a stop with muffled screeches. The doors split, and I moved along with the throng of people exiting the car. Bone tired, but I was going to a small rally straight from work. I'd been picked up as one of the subcontractors for a new construction project and being one of only three welders chosen, fourteen hour days were becoming the norm. Still, as a valued foot soldier of the brotherhood, no matter how exhausted I was, I never missed a meeting.

I trudged to the exit and onto the street. Moving from the shadows to the brighter rays of the late afternoon sun, blinded me for a second until my eyes adjusted. I pulled my cell free to check the time as I continued down the sidewalk. There was enough time to grab a quick bite from a convenience store before I was to meet Bruno and the gang. A sandwich or something would tide me over until I found a place to lay my head.

There was a little corner store a block ahead. I increased my pace, and walked through the open doors of the tiny market. A spicy scent permeated the air. There was a towel head behind the counter.

Stay or go?

It was rare to find an American owned market anymore. Grumbles rose from my stomach; I still needed to eat. I stalked up the tight aisles to the small refrigerated shelves and snatched up a sandwich container. Moving right along, I opened a cooler door and grabbed a cheap bottle of pop. I spun around and came face to face with *her*.

For a minute, I didn't know what to say. A myriad of nonsensical words flitted through my mind, my tongue stuck to the roof of my mouth. I opened my mouth with a faint snap. "What the hell are you doing here?" I blurted out.

She raised a hand and waved. "Hi."

I glanced around. We were too close to the meeting place. She shouldn't, couldn't be seen with me. I didn't utter another word, pressing my lips together. I walked away.

"What's your name?" She followed.

This girl was going to get killed. Worse, get me killed. I paused. *Wait*, why did it matter? She was nothing to me but a non-white entity. No one that I had a reason to worry about. It was her; she had no reason to be in my space—no fucking reason to be on this side of town. Still, I would warn her. "Don't follow me," I growled and dropped the items in my hand on a shelf before rushing past her. If she didn't listen then whatever happened to her was her fault.

"Wait." She gripped my elbow.

I gazed down at her, waiting for the repulsion, the hate I felt for everyone other than my own kind to roar through me.

Nothing.

I peered down at her fingers. Slim digits, her nails were long and had some elaborate design on them. All the women I knew didn't really sport fake nails, and they were usually short. They worked, and to keep a manicure was a costly habit to maintain when living paycheck to paycheck.

"Hey Brothe—" Bruno stood in the entrance of the store. His eyebrows slowly climbed up his forehead.

"Get your hand off me," I growled under my breath. This wasn't good for me or her. I brushed her hand away.

"What's going on here, Dachs?" A slow, wicked smile raised the corners of Bruno's mouth.

Son of a bitch.

I put some distance between me and the black girl. "Just some monkey trying to get my attention. You know I am a good-looking guy and all." A deep chuckle rumbled from my belly and through my lips. "Seems even shitty colored niggers want a taste of me." I clutched my crotch and laughed louder.

Bruno joined in laughing too. "Youse ain't the only one. Huh, blackie?" Then lower, more menacing. "I bet you got a lot of monkey sisters."

A look of pure horror crept across her face. Brackets framed her lips and her nostrils flared. Perhaps it was anger. Regardless, if Bruno was around, others were sure to follow, and she didn't need to be here when they did. I stepped in front of her, drawing my friend's attention. "Ain't it about time for the rally? Let's go." I shoved Bruno back.

"We got time." Bruno shuffled back, sidestepped my push and moved around me. "Why don't we go somewhere quiet? The three of us." He winked at me.

I already knew where this was going. "Why bother with her, when we have beautiful white women attending the rally with us? I won't bring the taint of that anywhere with me."

Bruno stared at the colored girl, his gaze roving up and down her body. My buddy wasn't answering me. Bruno was my best friend and one of the most brutal men I knew. There was still an open warrant out for him in New Jersey for attempted murder, after he beat a man into a coma. An urgency was building within me, making my stomach roil, and I wasn't sure why.

Finally, Bruno nodded slowly.

"Leave now, little niggeress," I tossed the words over my shoulder. It was the only thing I could do to save her.

What the hell am I thinking?

She eased away so quietly, I had to glance over my shoulder to make sure she moved.

"We ain't got to fuck her to have fun with her," Bruno grumbled, excitement lighting his eyes. His tongue darted out his mouth as he licked his lips.

Fuck.

My stomach dropped. I closed the gap between us and clutched his bicep. "It's broad-fucking-daylight. You are wanted. It's one thing to handle business in the dark of night. Too many witnesses around, Brother." I tipped my head toward the camel faced clerk behind the counter. "We can catch her another time." Did my friend hear the urgency in my tone?

Bruno inched back. His nostrils flared, and his gaze never left the blackie who dared to follow me.

I grabbed his chin and twisted his head to face me. "Save it for tonight for the rally."

"Yeah." Bruno's gaze focused on me, his grin growing wider. "There is always next time." He spun around and practically sulked through the exit.

"Maybe," I muttered, following him out of the store. I wouldn't, no couldn't look back. Watching her would give rise to thoughts I shouldn't have—questions I don't want answered. She'd been warned. That was all I could do for her. I caught myself gazing over my shoulder, anyway, before I trotted the few steps to catch up with Bruno.

$$7$$

HARPER

I had no words. Shock kept me speechless and motionless as both men quickly made to exit the store. The big brute of an asshole pushed through the door first. His head was bare but the black swastika tattoo that took up the entire back of his skull told me all I needed to know about who and what he was.

Asshole!

Dachs. What the fuck kind of name was that? German? That's what the asshole had called him. How dare he tell me to leave? How dare either of them. Then anger took root, replacing my initial shock and fear. I finally regained my senses and took a step forward to tell him exactly that. Dachs turned in my direction and slightly shook his head. There was a look in his eyes, like he was asking me not to say or do anything.

What the fuck?

I still stepped forward. Was he a skinhead too? Sounded like it. I have run into a racist or two, but in my circle, it's usually behind the scenes—never to my face. In my world, money is green and most don't care where they get it from. I've seen a few neo- Nazis but not close enough to touch. When those asswipes invaded UVA, I had a few friends who were from Charlottesville; some of them had family and friends there, black and white, and went there to protest the hate marches. No one close to me was a racist, although there were a few on campus who had questionable views. But no one—no one told me where I could or could not go. Not in my goddamn country, regardless of who is or isn't President. Those come and go; my rights are mine.

I took another step in the direction of the door, but the man behind the counter called out to me and got my attention.

"You know those guys? They bad men. If they threaten you, I call the cops."

I smiled at the man. He had a heavy East Indian accent. "Thank you, but I'm fine. And no, I don't know them. Do you?"

"The one with the tattoo on his head, he come in here all the time. Him and his friends. But this the first time I see the other one. But, he just like all the rest. They hold their meeting of hate not too far from here. A few weeks ago a friend of mine was badly beaten because he was the wrong shade at the wrong place at the wrong time."

I gasped. "That's horrible. Did he go to the police?"

The man nodded. "Of course. But he never saw their faces. They threw a bag over his head and beat him all the while calling him dirty names and telling him to go back where he came from. His parents were born in America, so was he. Where is he supposed to go back to—Maryland where he was born?" He chuckled, but it wasn't one of mirth. "They gone now, but you might want to call a cab. This isn't a very good neighborhood for a nice young woman of any color to be walking around when the sun goes down and sometimes when it's still bright."

I smiled. "Thank you. But..." I glanced outside and didn't see Dachs or his friend on the sidewalk. As much as I wanted to go after them and tell them a thing or two, I let common sense rule me. I needed to process this. The look in the second man's eyes wasn't one of hate; maybe hate was there, but so was lust. It made my skin crawl. Dachs never looked at me like that. I'd give him that much. I'd never encountered anything like this—wasn't sure how to handle it either. I pulled out my phone and called an Uber.

On impulse, I'd gotten off the train, hoping to be able to talk to the guy I'd been seeing for the last few days. The only reason I'd decided to follow him was because of that look that had passed between us on the train. It had not been my imagination. There was something, some kind of pull drawing me to him, and he wasn't immune either. I had good business instincts, maybe not so good people ones. I just had to go talk to him in the store. *Ha!* Not much of a conversation, and what little there had been, was not good at all. Talk about culture shock.

I walked out of the store and looked up and down the street, hoping for a glimpse of Dachs. Even now, why was I looking for him? He was probably a skinhead too, but his head was not shaved. What did it matter? Shaved head or not, did he hate people different from himself too? I got in the car, unable to keep re-running everything in my head. I took a deep breath. The thought of such ignorance made me sad—that you would purposely close yourself off from the vast majority of the human race. When it comes down to it, it's our differences that make us interesting.

I pulled out my phone and called Serena.

"Hey, girlie, whaddup?"

"You'll never believe what just happened." I told her everything, and she was pissed.

"I'll jump in my car right now with my baseball bat and knock some frigging sense into those Nazi sons of bitches. Who the fuck do they think they are? Let's see if a bash to the head would help enlighten them for a change."

I had to chuckle over her outrage. It helped to calm me

down. Even though I knew she wasn't quite kidding. One time, Serena and I were on our way to a party and heard muffled cries coming from the edges of the parking lot. We saw a girl being literally dragged into the woods. Serena screamed and ran toward them; she had about a million keys on her key ring and held it in her fist. The guy took one look at the crazy woman descending on him, released the girl and took off. But, Serena didn't stop. I only paused long enough to make sure the girl was alright, screamed at her to call 911 and took off after my friend— not surprised to find Serena had caught the guy; she'd tackled him from behind and was punching him on the head with her keys while she straddled his back. Before he could turn over I joined her, and we kept him pinned until the cops came. So, when she said she'd go looking for them, I had no doubt.

"Say the word, and I'm there," she said.

Now normally, Serena was one of the sweetest, kindest people I knew. She never started a fight, but she'll finish it. Just don't get her mad by picking on someone weaker, and she was loyal to those closest to her.

"Nah. But you know, the weirdest thing is, I think he was actually trying to defuse the situation. I had no doubt in my mind his friend would have tried to hurt me. And if he'd laid a hand on me, I'd have looked for the nearest glass bottle to defend myself. But Dachs—"

"Wait, Dachs! His name is Dachs? Is that first or last? Sounds German. Damn, he really is one of those 'heil Hitler' freaks."

"I think so. But I...I think he was really trying to get the other one away from me. When I'd started to follow them out of the store, he shook his head at me, wrapped his arm around his friend's shoulder and guided him away from the door."

"Still don't make him a friend."

"No. No it doesn't."

"Well maybe it's best to just stay the hell away from him. I don't want to have to kill anyone. Sounds like a good time to take a break and get out of town. Isn't there a holiday coming up?"

"Maybe."

"Well let this be a lesson for you, there are other good looking men out there that are not deliberately ignorant or lacking in common sense. Well at least a few."

"Ya think?"

I YAWNED, waiting for the train. I'd been up most of the night thinking and rethinking over what had happened. I'd stared at the pictures I'd snuck of him. *Dachs.* Serena was right. I needed to stay away from this guy and his issues. Violence was not really my thing. And except for that one time sophomore year, never touched my life. The kind of hate, the kind he had for others, I had no interest in whatsoever. They can stay in their little ignorant boxes and I'll roam the world.

Oh, I know shit happens but this was the first time anything even remotely close invaded my bubble since it was directed at me. I was still sad that this man wasn't who I thought he was. Then again I wasn't sure what I'd thought. But not a damn in your face racist! Now I was pissed again. Pissed at the narrow mindedness of some people. Which is why I was truly on a mission today. I wasn't about to just let this go. There comes a time when you have to stand up or go meekly to the back of the bus. I don't do meek or buses. I didn't have class today. Even if I did, I would miss it. I had things to say to this Dachs—up close and personal.

Funny, how after a while, I still can't get used to the smell. I had no backpack, just my mid-sized, Longchamp cross-body, I grasped the strap in front of me as I got on the train. This time it wasn't too crazy, only a few people were standing. Most of the seats were taken. I'd gotten on at the front of the train, that's where I usually saw him, it was where I'd first seen him. But, I didn't see him this time. I felt a weight settle in my chest at his absence. Not sure if it was because I couldn't tell him where he could shove his stupid, ignorant-ass ideology, or if it was because I just wanted to see him again. What the hell was wrong with me?

Maybe I just needed a vacation and to get my head on straight as Serena had suggested. There was a long holiday weekend coming up, and I'd go out of town with Serena. Dad had a rental property in Punta Cana we could use for a few days, grab some sun, get out of this cold and away from skinhead assholes.

Instead of sitting at the first available seat or getting off the train at the next stop and turning my ass around, I found myself going into the second car. That's where I saw him. He sat against the window, facing away from me. The seat across from him was empty. I made my way over to it. My heart thundered in my ears, drowning out the screech of the wheels on the train tracks. I didn't care. I've never run from anything in my life, and I would be damned if I ran now. He wanted a fight, he got one. I sat down and crossed my arms over my chest. He glanced up and our eyes locked; his at first seemed surprised but then narrowed in suspicion.

"Dachs. What the hell kind of name is that?" He started to open his mouth to speak, but I held up my hand, stopping him. "Oh no. You had your say yesterday. It's my turn now. My name's Harper Hodges, by the way, not niggeress or blackie or anything else. And, if you ever refer to me as a 'monkey' again, I will go ape shit up your ass. What is wrong with you people? Do you not have a brain in your head and know how to use it?" I held up my hand again, letting him know I was not done and told him so. "Still my turn. You and your friends need a serious reality check. I am a part of this world; I and others like me, others different from you, are not going anywhere. So, get over yourselves. We all crawled out of the same pond. I almost thought I wanted to get to know you. That you were someone worth knowing. That I might actually like you." I leaned forward to make sure I got my point across. "I was wrong—not something that happens very often."

"I know I told you to stay the fuck away from me." He cocked his head, quietly staring at me.

"Don't cuss at me, it's rude, and I go where I please. And, this seat has my name engraved on it."

"Show me where you carved your name?" The deep grumble of his voice rose from his chest. "Do you have any idea how easy it would be for me to kill you and leave your body slumped in the seat you claim?" A wicked smile lifted the side of his mouth. "One less *nigger* in the world."

I blinked. Then, I couldn't help myself. I busted out laughing. Not the silly girlie kinda giggle some girls do but a full on belly laugh where my eyes were tearing up a bit. It was either laugh at his stupidity or hit him. Laughter it was. Taking a deep breath, I pulled a marker out of the front of my bag and carved my name into the seat. With a wicked smile of my own, I looked into his eyes and said, "Can you read? Or do you need me to tell you my name again. I would *love* to see you try that because there would certainly be one less Neanderthal infecting the planet. Oh, is that word too big for you? How about simpleton? You use that word with me again and only one of us will be walking off this train, and she's the one wearing pointed heels."

8

DACHS

The black girl was bold, and I could have gotten up at any time, but I was curious. The urge to beat the shit out of her didn't consume me like I was sure it might. I would never admit this to anyone else, but I have never lied to myself. I wanted to hear what she had to say. She was staring at me, expectantly, almost like she hoped I would dispute something, anything she said. There was one point I would clear up before I left.

"Dachs is the name my mother gave me. It was my grandfather's name and my great-great grandfather's name. There is history and power in my name, and that is something you may never understand." I scooted to the edge of my seat. "Don't ever follow me again. I will not say this again."

She kicked a leg up making sure I got a good look at her pointed heel. "I'm not finished."

I stared at her. It was cute, how she thought she was in control. A long sigh blew past my lips. When did she become cute? It could happen; *monkeys are cute.* Now was not the time to think too hard about that.

"I give less than a damn." She was trouble, no doubt. But there was something about her. Her tenacity—maybe. Anyone else, knowing what I am, would have run away. Instead, this... girl came looking for me. There might just be something wrong with the darkie. Cuteness did not excuse blackness, after all. Why the fuck was I still sitting across from her?

"I don't care what you think." She held my gaze.

I was reminded of those little dogs that couldn't bite worth shit, and yet, they kept nipping at your heels. Her stubbornness was epic. I eased back in my seat. She felt the need to express herself. I would listen for now. A grudging respect because no one listened to my arguments. Often trying to force their opinion on me, much like she was doing right now. Trying to make someone else see my point of view was tiresome. It was also why so many brothers resorted to violence...the frustration of not being heard. Sure, there were the Brunos that were part of the group. Men and women, extremist, who were zealous in their views, but not all of us were violent criminals that social media often made us out to be. A lot of my brethren just wanted a clear delineation between the races. A stay in your own lane type deal, and most of us kept to our own, choosing to be heard through networking and literature.

"Aren't you scared, little girl?"

I am no Bruno. I craved no urge to kill anyone, in spite of what I told her. I just wanted a clear separation of the races. Like a line in the sand, if everyone played in their own sandbox, violence wasn't necessary.

"What is there to be afraid of?" Harper pressed her lips together and tilted her chin up.

A snort escaped past my lips before I could call it back. Encouraging her nonsense wasn't something I wanted to do. This Harper kid needed to understand how things worked in the real world. "You should be. I'm no fairytale villain. I'm the real thing and you're not ready for me."

"You're an obnoxious and hateful asshole."

"Yet, you keep following me."

She crossed her arms under her breasts. "I've never been one to look the other way. You need to know you're wrong. And I'm not afraid to tell you that to your face."

Her obnoxiousness was...interesting and exhausting. Almost like she wanted to fight. "What's right or wrong is objective. History is written by whoever is in charge." Since joining the National Movement for the Advancement of White People in my junior year of high school, I'd heard it all. "What I want is for you to stop trying to force your ideals on me. I have nothing to say to you, and if you didn't follow me, my ideals would not have been spouted at you. You are immature and entitled. I don't like you. This fact goes beyond the color of your skin—a trait most of you *monkeys* seem to share." I was tired. Yeah that was it. I am exhausted, and she wasn't worth the energy I needed to work up to beat some sense into her head.

The arguments boiled down to a simple matter: with all the privileges given to minorities, white people could no longer compete. Jobs, basic housing, education, we were losing ground on all fronts because *those* people weren't happy with their lives and to them nothing was ever fair. The girl in front of me proved it. I gave her every opportunity to walk away, and still, she wasn't satisfied. Maybe if I had let Bruno have his way with her, she would have a better understanding of what it means to stay the fuck out of my way.

"People are people. There is no fundamental difference between them; history and biology proves that. Your ancestors were right next to mine swinging from trees. And, you are a jerk!"

Why was she still talking? I gazed at her through narrowed eyes. A better question was why did she sound hurt? Her little temper tantrum shouldn't bother me. It was obvious we came from two very different places—worlds that should have never collided. Did she even realize she had such an earnest look on her face? Locks of her hair danced around her head with every movement she made.

Were they soft?

A hint of red flushed her cheeks. The urge to touch her face slammed through me. I needed to leave, but I wanted to stay. This woman was sin and everything the brotherhood was against. I should find her very being an offense...but she isn't, not really. What did the Prof call it?

Jungle fever.

The urge to taste the forbidden. Like that damn apple Eve talked Adam into biting. This woman was like a virus. Hell, I could very well already be infected.

"Save the tantrum for your parents. Why are you following me?" I didn't want to hear the bullshit reasons she was using. There was more to her story. I sighed. For reasons I wasn't sure I wanted to explore, her answers, I needed to hear them.

Harper seemed to hesitate before replying. "I told you."

I shook my head. "There is always more to a story." I learned a long time ago there are always three truths: Their side, my side and what is actually happening.

"Why?" Her words were a whisper. "*Why* do you have a problem with other races?"

This was a question my mom had asked me a hundred—no, a thousand times. The answer had been drummed into my head since joining the movement. "If God wanted us to mix, he wouldn't have separated us to begin with." It was the proven truth. The Prof, the founder of the NMAWP, had shown scientific documentation any time anyone asked him to prove the point.

She frowned. "How stupid can you be?"

When faced with the truth, people were all the same. Disappointment at Harper's response fluttered along my nerves. She didn't want to understand me. They always had the same answer. Instead of disputing what I said with evidence, I was mocked. Like Prof said, probably because there was no rebuttal. Really, it was time to go. Still, I stayed. "That's the best answer you can come up with? Questioning my intelligence."

Her eyes widened briefly before her mask of indignation returned. "Yes, when dumb actions are combined with idiotic statements."

I cocked my head to the side. This wasn't even a decent conversation. It was an attack. My fascination for her tapered down quickly. God, but she needed to stay in her bubble. The real world might be too much for her. "I haven't followed you or encouraged you to come and find me. I have no interest in a woman that isn't white."

Other than the occasional fuck with Becky, I was busy. I hadn't bothered to find a replacement for my friend. Women were complicated, and I had shit to do.

Between work, tech classes and rallies, taking the train was the only time I had a few moments to myself, and now, even *that* was invaded. My stop was announced over the speaker. I was leaving a stupidly innocent girl among wolves, and it somehow felt wrong leaving her to travel alone.

There is something seriously wrong with me.

I didn't ask her to find me.

Get her home. You will be done with her then. Make it clear that she needs to stay away from me.

The train rolled to a stop and the doors slid open.

She'd been alright so far, walk away.

My cell rumbled in my pocket. I pulled it free. "Yeah." My gaze never left her.

"Prof wants us to meet. You need to come," Bruno grunted.

"I'll be there in a bit." I ended the call and rose. Without saying a word, I slipped through the exit. I wasn't comfortable leaving her by herself. In a split second, I made an unconscious decision. Before it dawned on me, I was moving away from the exit. I sprinted down the next car over and squeezed through the door as they closed.

Why was I lying?

If Bruno suspected it had anything to do with the black girl he'd run into yesterday, his interest would be reignited. That was dangerous. Not just for her but for everyone. My best friend's hair trigger temper had gotten him into problems before. My cell buzzed in my fist. I answered without speaking.

"Damn. I wasn't finished talking. I told you, Brother, quit that job. What do you need it for? We could run a few errands and make what we need. Dedicate all our time to the brotherhood like the soldiers we should be."

I grabbed a seat in the front and gazed through the glass. "Hmm." This wasn't the first time Bruno urged me to cut all ties with the world and just follow the movement. That didn't exactly feel right either. I wanted options. Furthering the movement required education and money. I couldn't get one without the other. I ignored Bruno's comment. "It will take me about an hour to get there. You woke me up, and I just missed my stop. I'll get off at the next stop and Uber."

"Ooo, do that. I hope you get a fun driver, someone other than white. I found my bat, that one I brought with me from Jersey, and cleaned it up. I need to baptize it here in Boston."

"You're a freak." I chuckled. "I don't think you will get that lucky." I wasn't in the mood to fight. I would make sure my driver was white before I got in the car. It would save me any headaches later on. "I'll see you later." I ended the call. My gaze drifted to the next car. Follow the black girl home, and then get to my meeting, sounded too stalker like, so maybe just make sure she doesn't get harassed on the train. It is a sound plan. I scooted down in the seat. Why the hell was I pretending to be a good man?

9

HARPER

I watched Dachs get off the train and sighed. I couldn't really understand my emotions. I was angry, sad, and yet, exhilarated. I loved arguing with him. If I didn't love numbers I'd have probably gone into law. I enjoyed a good argument. Still, what the hell was wrong with me following that man and confronting him like that? Yet, for all his talk of danger, while I have no doubt his friends might be, I wasn't so sure about him. He was different, but the crap he sprouted had to go. I should probably do as he says and just leave him the hell alone, stay in my lane and let him stay in his. There was a tightness in my chest at that thought, but I did what I had to and regretted nothing.

I got off at the next stop, not sure where it was really and had zero interest in catching another train to take me home. Instead, I took the stairs to the upper level.

I saw a couple of cabs but other people grabbed them. Didn't matter, I took out my phone and called an Uber. It was only a few minutes away, so I didn't have to wait long. I moved to the edge of the sidewalk and waited. I zipped my jacket up, it was getting colder, and glanced around. Definitely, not the kind of neighborhood I wanted to be in at night or anytime of day for very long. Thankfully, the Uber pulled up just as I noticed a pair of guys with bandannas on their heads eyeing me. I opened the car door and got inside, breathing a sigh of relief. I glanced over my shoulder at the men and was very glad I wasn't standing out there for very long. Funny the way those men gave off dangerous vibes the way they eyed me like I was prey, whereas I never felt like that with Dachs. Could he be dangerous? He claimed he was, and I believed him; while my feelings toward him were conflicting, I never feared him.

I'D SPENT the day catching up on my work, and the night was mine. I took a taxi and met Serena and Steven for drinks near Serena's townhouse she shared with Steven. I walked into the bar, and it was live band night. I'd forgotten the place was loud, but it was just what I needed to not be in my head any more than I already was.

"Hey, bitch," Serena said as I approached the table. She stood up and embraced me.

"Back at ya. Looking good." And she was. While I was on the shorter side, Serena was tall—well taller than my 5'4" frame by three inches in her bare feet. Tonight, we were both wearing heels, and she was still taller. The red jumper she wore hugged her in all the right places.

"Hey, beautiful," Steve said, standing up and kissing me on the cheek.

"Hey, beautiful, yourself," I smiled. If the man wasn't gay, I'd have already been all over him but this was even better. He was my best friend; they both were.

Steve flagged the waiter over and ordered my favorite martini—chocolate of course. "Thanks, just what I needed."

"What's up?" Steve asked. "Rough day?."

I hesitated, but I had to tell them. Serena had already told Steve about my earlier run in with Dachs. I told them about my most recent one.

"Wow!" Steve said. "Gurl, this guy must be *hot* if you're chasing him and putting up with that bullshit."

I pulled out my phone and showed him some pictures. Steven's mouth dropped open. He didn't say a thing, just took the phone away from me and scrolled through it.

"I think that's the first time he's ever been speechless," Serena said, laughing.

Steve handed me back my phone. "Okay, okay I get the attraction; he's got that whole 'magnetism' thing going." He shivered. "I might have followed him myself. But hon, it's not worth the headache. This dude got looks but no brains."

I shook my head. "That's just it, other than the crap he sprouts, I'm not so sure he's stupid. There's intelligence in those eyes."

"I'll give you that; those eyes are made to dream about, and I bet they're even more intense up close and personal, but you still need to be careful around him."

"Steve's right," Serena agreed.

I'm glad I didn't quite tell them everything—like, the fact he threatened me, but I didn't take it seriously. Besides, I threatened him too. No, I never once thought he'd harm me. But, were they right? Maybe I needed to be careful with him, definitely around his friends, but with him, I didn't know?

Our drinks came, and after the waiter left, I took a big sip. The alcohol hit my bloodstream and had me feeling much better. "I don't think either of you have anything to worry about. I doubt I'll see him again. I suspect he'll make it a point to avoid me."

"Then, that's good," Serena replied.

"Yeah," Steve agreed.

Yet, I knew if I saw him first, I wouldn't be able to resist talking to him. Let him walk away, if he could. It seemed I didn't want to.

~

MONDAY I WAS BACK on the T. I still wasn't used to the stench, but I was better prepared for it. I had a Hermes scarf wrapped around my neck, and I'd dabbed a bit of my favorite perfume on it, *Joy*.

Every now and then, I'd lower my nose in an attempt to avoid any unpleasant odors. It worked about half the time. But, I could do nothing about my other senses. I just hoped I didn't become half deaf from all the noise from the machines and the masses of humanity.

I got the first train car; it was crowded but I didn't see him. I kept moving to the second one which had a few empty seats. I thought about heading for the third one, but it seemed crowded, and I really didn't feel like standing. I sat down in the first available seat, so I was facing the front of the train. I saw a guy walking up the aisle eyeing me, so I made sure and moved over to the aisle seat and plunked my backpack down in the seat next to the window. For good measure I put my feet up against the seat next to me. Could I make it any more obvious that he was NOT going to sit there next to me.

He kept walking, and once he passed, I put my feet down.

The train pulled off, and I turned to pull my phone out of the front pocket of my bag.

"Move."

I glanced up to tell the asshole to keep moving, when I realized it wasn't the asshole I'd been expecting. Yet, I picked up my bag and did exactly that. Taking the inside seat and giving him the end. My heart skipped a beat at the sight of him and his proximity. I wanted to smile in triumph.

"Wow! Not even a please? Did your mother not teach you manners either?"

"I respect those that respect me."

"I see it didn't work so well."

He shrugged, settling into the seat.

"Why are you sitting next to me? I thought you told me to leave you alone, yet, here you are." Whatever the hell was going on, I wasn't the only one feeling it. In many ways he was right; we are both very different. But, it's those differences that makes us interesting. I didn't think he could forget me either, like I couldn't forget him. I knew it probably irritated him to no end. I challenged him, as he challenged me. Time would tell if that would be a good thing or bad. But, I wanted to hear what he had to say.

10

DACHS

She was staring at me.

This was the last time little Harper and I would meet. A long sigh blew through my lips. It was safer for both of us that way. I turned off my cell and shoved it into my pocket. "How long are we going to play this game?" How else could I get it through her head; she couldn't look for me.

I'd looked up and saw her sitting, claiming seats. She was bold considering she was a T newbie. The stranger that stared at her would circle back if there were no free seats in the next car. Just like last time, the unease of seeing her alone roared through me.

Only a couple days ago, I watched as she exited the train and caught an Uber to who knew where. I figured it was the last time I would see her. Despite her color, grudgingly I had to admit her tenacity was impressive.

"I wasn't—I didn't look for you?" she snapped.

"You don't look like the type. Maybe I'm wrong. You seem honest, at least to your truth. I'm a little *disappointed*." To add emphasis to my words, I rose and leaned into her space. Caging her with my arms and getting into her face. We were so close I could count the freckles peppering the bridge of her nose. Her sweet scent wafted to my nose. I was reminded of fresh flowers. The urge to close my eyes, and soak it in, was overwhelming. I pressed my lips together in a refusal to give in. This back and forth between us needed to stop before someone got hurt. "I am not a good man," I grumbled more to remind myself than the woman—no—the *thing* in front of me was off limits. The train stopped and riders moved around exiting the cab.

"Transit Authorities are patrolling the cars." The baritone rumble came from my side. I glanced up and met the cold, brown eyes of Gage Clarke as he stared down at me; his face an unreadable mask of indifference.

I straightened and returned his gaze. A few years older, and originally from the Boston area as the city became more integrated, his family chose to leave and start a new branch of NMAWP in a small town in upstate New York. As second in command of that chapter, every couple of months he ran errands for the Prof. Rumors swirled around the group that they were true family, the Prof's nephew, but it wasn't something anyone discussed openly.

Gage was a big bastard, with a short temper and a long reach —tall, broad shouldered and muscular. His fists were the size of small plates, and there was one occasion during a jump in, I witnessed him fracture a man's jaw with one punch. He had nondescript features, with dark hair and eyes. If not for his size, he could easily mix into a crowd and get lost among the people. Never uttering more than a few words, it was hard to tell what he may be thinking. He was not an enemy I wanted to have. Just how much had he heard? "You're back?" Talking with Gage was like playing verbal chess.

Gage pushed past me and claimed the seat across from mine.

I peered over at him. The asshole wasn't giving anything away. I shifted around, dropped into the seat beside him and stared ahead at the woman that unknowingly might have just signed my death warrant. To look at Gage for any length of time would be like admitting some sort of guilt.

Harper's gazed darted between me and Gage. Her lips were pressed together in a firm line, and for a brief moment, her nose flared. Tension grew around us, blanketing me in a cocoon of hyper awareness. The obnoxious woman couldn't be here. She was a distraction, and her mouth would get us killed, if Gage wasn't already planning our deaths. I eased forward and twisted to watch Gage, while I partially blocked his view of her.

Officers squeezed through the passengers passing us.

"You can't touch her here." Gage calmly, quietly uttered the words. "What the hell you thinking? I thought you were smarter than Bruno."

The barb stung. I had no blood thirst. A burst of relief followed; maybe his take on things wasn't what I thought. Or, they were words uttered to make me comfortable. I stared unblinkingly at Gage. Let the games begin. "I was offering advice."

Gage leaned forward and rested his elbows on his knees. He cocked his head and stared past me at the black girl as he locked his fingers. "Leave. Now."

I would not directly look at her, and instead, glanced over my shoulder. "You heard him, little niggeress; get out of here. You got lucky today," I grumbled. If she said anything, I knew it would be hell getting her off the train. I kept my mouth shut, silently willing her to do the same. Time stretched on.

Gage shifted, and I moved to counter his position, completely turning to face him in my seat. A litany of words was spouted behind me in a flurry of movement.

"Fuck you," she spoke up, loudly as she pushed past me, her hip knocking my shoulder.

I sat back and watched as she pressed through the throng of

riders surrounding us. The train ground to a stop. Commuters traded places, entering and exiting the car. I could no longer see the woman I felt the need to protect.

"You got a taste for the forbidden?" Gage slowly turned his head and faced me.

I held his gaze and exhaled. "You let her go. I'm wondering if you have an affection for niggers?"

A deep, rusty chuckle erupted past his lips. "You're smarter than Prof's average minions."

"I'm no one's minion." White pride was about individuality. The idea that many people with the same thoughts were more powerful than a single person fighting to maintain the equality we are quickly losing. "I am just one of a lot like minded people protecting our rights."

Gage combed his fingers through his hair, pushing the strands back. A hint of a smirk lifted a corner of his mouth. "Not when you associate with the enemy."

"A little harassment didn't hurt her." I grinned in return. "It was fun."

"Interesting."

I didn't like the way that sounded.

"Prof know you got a taste for darkies?" Gage continued.

I eased back into my seat and settled in as the train resumed. Our little headquarters was a few stops ahead. The action gave me time to think. "Whatever you think you know about me —prove it."

"All I have to do is mention it. Prof will take my word."

My heart pounded in my chest. Death wasn't something I feared, but what would happen to *her* if Prof put the word out she was someone he was looking for? "Do it!" I challenged, taking a gamble.

More rusty barks of laughter escaped through Gage's lips. "I like you. I hope the time doesn't come that I have to kill you."

"If one of us ever has to die…it won't be me." I shrugged. A grudging respect has been established between us. Everything would have to play out now. Time would tell exactly what Gage was thinking through his actions and staying away from the little, black woman is more important than ever. I exhaled slowly.

"Keep your bad habits better hidden, and we won't have to find out who will die first."

"White Power," I uttered as I closed my eyes to feign sleep. This world—my world was feeling more and more suffocating.

11

HARPER

For the love of God; what the fuck!

I was done—done and then done again. What the hell kind of seriously messed up friends does this dude have? Were they all as assholey? That's what I get for riding public transportation. From now on, my plan was to stay in my own socioeconomic atmosphere with likeminded people. I was seriously ill equipped to deal with that kind of bigotry and hatred. Seriously, who in their right minds could?

Unfortunately, the universe was playing some majorly twisted joke on me. My frigging car wouldn't start the next day, and Justin was still out of town, Serena was at her part-time job and Steve was already pulling into the parking lot at school.

Damnit anyway.

I pulled out my phone. "Dad."

"Sorry, Harper, it's Teresa. Your father isn't available right now. I can take a message or maybe there's something I can help you with?"

'Yes, you can put my damn father on the phone' is what I wanted to say but refrained.

Play nice.

"No, that's fine. I'll call him later."

"You sure? Is everything okay?"

"Yes, I'm fine. Tell him I'll call him later." Then, I hung up the phone, not wanting to be on a minute longer than necessary. I sure as hell was not going to tell her to let him know about my car problems—*again*. The second time in a few weeks, two too many times. It was most definitely time for a new car.

I had my car towed off to the mechanics, catching a ride with the driver, hoping they could have me back on the road in no time. That would be a 'no.' I was not feeling any happier when the mechanic told me they'd call me in a couple of hours after they'd run diagnostics on it. He didn't believe it was the same problem I'd been having last time.

Yeah right!

They probably took one look at the car, one at me and saw dollar signs—*cha ching!* One brainless female, and suddenly, there are all these *extra* problems with the damn car that never existed before I took it to them to begin with. I should have taken it to the damn dealer, but it was too far from my condo— not that they're any better, just more expensive.

I walked into the lobby area and called an Uber, the app showed the closest one was twenty minutes out. What the H? I tried Lyft. Same thing. I stared at my phone. What in the world was going on?

"If you're trying to catch a Lyft or Uber, don't bother. There's some large convention in town tying them up, and there's been an accident that's messing with traffic."

"Thanks," I said to the service guy who'd spoken to me. "Any chance for a loaner?"

"Sorry, we don't really do that here."

I sighed, dreading what was coming. I left the shop and walked down to the T to catch the train. I only had one class today, and it was going to be cutting it close. If you got there late, the professor wouldn't let you in, and he marks absences. This might be my first one, but I had to try.

It was a big train; I shouldn't have any trouble avoiding seeing anyone on there I didn't want to. To make sure of it as the train pulled in, I moved down to the end of the platform; so by the time the train stopped, I stood before the last car and got on there.

It wasn't too crowded, but I made sure and sat next to someone who was seated next to the window. I placed my bag down on the floor and leaned back. I took a deep breath and closed my eyes, wanting to block out the sights and sounds of everyone around me. I tried to take shallow breaths because I will never get used to the scent of stale body odor and week old food. But, as the train slowed to approach the next stop, I felt the person seated beside me move, as though they were getting up. I didn't bother to open my eyes. But something made me.

Perhaps it was the fact I could feel someone else take the seat across from me—or self-preservation, not sure, maybe both. Suddenly I found myself looking at the man I'd been doing my damndest now to avoid or ignore. Yet, the way my face heated and my body flushed at his presence, told me that was a lie.

I guess I'd been right all along. We can't seem to ignore each other. Still, I wasn't going to make it easy for him—not in my nature. I was truly tired of all his posturing and bullshit. This time, I hadn't been the one to go looking for him. No question he sought me out. Had he seen me walk by the other cars before and followed me unto this one? It gave me both a stalker kind of feeling, but at the same time, something more. Perhaps, for the same reasons I'd gotten on the train the last few times, if not this time, looking for him.

I didn't hesitate. I stared hard at him. If I could growl, I would. "What do you want?" I glanced past him looking for one of his bastard friends. "What? No sidekicks this time? So, you're all alone on the train with little old me?"

"I have never had an entourage. Never will."

"Whatever! I don't need your bullshit or your crazy ass friends either."

"I don't remember asking you if you did. I don't remember initiating any of our freaky 'meet ups.' You don't have sense to be afraid of me or my associates."

"What is there to be afraid of?" I tilted my chin up, daring him. In that moment, I realized I really wasn't afraid of him.

A snort escaped past his lips. "You should be. I keep telling you. I'm no fairytale villain, and you're not ready for me."

"You know you can be obnoxious and hateful."

"Yet, you follow me."

I shook my head. "Oh no. Not this time. You found me. But, you do need someone to tell you about yourself. You need to know you're wrong." The fact hurt my heart he couldn't see it.

"Why do you keep trying to force your beliefs on me? I didn't ask for them. I did not ask you to follow or contact me. You got a dose of reality, and you don't like it." He sighed, long and low. "I'm tired of fighting with someone who is constantly harping on her version of views, without constructively listening to mine."

I had to sit on my hands to stop myself from shaking some sense into his head. "People are people. Aside from the psychopaths, there is no fundamental difference between them. You are a jerk for not seeing that!" I tried my best to keep the hurt out of my voice, but it snuck out anyway. I couldn't help it; what he was stung. It shouldn't, but that didn't seem to matter. Even though we were arguing, there was this draw, something between us. I gave a damn; why can't he?

"It's obvious we come from two very different places—worlds that should have never collided," he said.

For a minute, he stared at the lock I'd just brushed back off my face. Did he want to touch it? My God, he leaned forward a bit like he wanted to, did I want him to? I leaned forward slightly to see what he'd do. Instead, he sat back and crossed his arms over his chest.

"Why are you following me?" This time, I asked the question.

He stared at me for a long moment before answering. "Yeah. I'm not."

We both knew he lied. He sought me out the same way I had him. I had wanted to know more about him. In truth, what I'd learned hadn't been good. Yet, in spite of everything, we were still talking. But, since I couldn't really explain it, I didn't really expect him to.

His gaze never left mine, and something in my core reacted because there was heat in that gaze. Not the hate kind, in contrast to what his words implied. The fact he sought me out this time, spoke louder than his words. The way he looked at me was one I recognized because I'd seen it in other men.

His phone dinged like he got a text. He checked it and replied. I was curious as to if it was a woman. Suddenly, I felt an overwhelming sense of jealousy, which only pissed me off.

He put his phone away.

I just stared at him.

"Where do you live?" he asked.

"Why?" I asked confused.

"I'll make sure you get home, or wherever you're going. Then, it's best if we stay away from each other. Let me remind you of what I told you before. I am not a good man."

I snorted. "Sure. Whatever you say." My heart never stopped hammering against my chest again at his nearness. His eyes were so damn blue. Like the waters in Horseshoe Bay Bermuda. Was he right? Was he like the Bermuda Triangle—dangerous to travel through? Would I lose myself if I kept staring at him? But, his eyes roamed over my face too. If either of us leaned forward, just a bit more, our lips would touch. With that thought, my gaze shifted to his mouth. His lower lip was slightly fuller than the upper one, which was nicely outlined with the slight mustache he sported and framed within his goatee.

I blinked. "Leakey," I blurted out.

"What?"

"You'd asked for proof, evidence to contradict your beliefs, Louis and Mary Leakey. Look 'em up. Do you read things other than what this 'Prof' recommends? Or, do you practice selective reading?" I glared at him.

"If it has nothing to do with the movement, it's not something I will concern myself with."

"So, deliberate ignorance?"

"Just me being *stupid* I suppose."

"You asked for evidence. I gave you a way to find it yourself. We all crawled out of the same pond. I'd love to be a fly on the wall and see your face when you read about them." I chuckled.

He frowned at me but glanced up as the train started again. I heard his softly spoken cuss word.

"Your stop?" I guessed.

"Where is your stop? Didn't we already pass it?"

"So, you know where I get off?" He said nothing, only stared at me. I checked my phone. "Damn. I only had one class today, and I missed it." I'd been so focused on him, I hadn't even noticed we'd past my stop.

"I don't have time for games, Harper. I'm getting off at the next stop, with or without you."

I sighed. "I live in Back Bay."

"Your family can afford that?"

"Not that it's any of your business, but I have a condo in Back Bay. My family lives in Beacon Hill."

"Get the fuck out of here. You kidding me? This is the shit

the Prof talks about. Affirmative fucking Action at work. Better jobs taken by undeserving fucking hacks. Of course, you people can do well. You have it easy. Meanwhile, hard working white men and women don't get into neighborhoods like that. How long did it take your people to crawl up out of federal housing?"

"First of all, I don't live in any low-income housing, never have. There isn't any that I know of in my neighborhood. If anyone built anything that's a set aside, trust me, the new owner fixes it up a bit and flips it for more than they paid for it. My father, I'm sure, also paid full price for the house I grew up in. I got into school because of my grades, you jerk. *GRADES.* Harvard takes nothing less than the best. I happen to be fucking smart."

He snorted.

"What? You applied and didn't get in?"

"Never had an interest to." The train slowed down, pulling into the next stop, and he stood. "You coming or not?"

"You don't have to see me home. I can take care of myself."

"Not if you're following guys like me around. I can't see how. Roaming around, the way you do, you need a keeper."

"Is that supposed to be you?"

He said nothing. Merely headed toward the door. I sat for a minute, wondering what the hell I was doing. But as soon as the door opened, I jumped up and followed him. He glanced at me and smirked.

"For the record, you followed me this time, not the other way around." I reminded him. He still hadn't really explained why he felt the need to follow me this time. Neither of us seemed quite ready to let the other go. I wondered who would be following whom next time.

Dachs stuck his hands in his pockets and glanced around.

I frowned. "You lost or something?"

"Nah."

I started to tell him I could just call a car, but I didn't. My curiosity was back in full force. I wanted to spend more time with him. I wanted to figure him out—what made him tick? I needed to understand why I was so attracted to him—why I needed to understand him and his hatred. I should be running in the other direction. Instead, I walked with him to the escalator and crossed over to the other side to take the train back to my part of the city. A man who was not good, as he'd claimed, would not have offered to make sure I got home safely. He was a puzzle I needed to figure out—either that or lose my damn mind.

He didn't say another word to me, but he seemed restless. He seemed to constantly continue to scan the area. Was he searching for someone? Then a thought occurred to me.

"Are you worried one of your ignorant friends will see you with me again?" I snorted. "Heaven forbid they kick you out of the Klan." I was so angry, my stomach clenched. The train pulled up. "You know what? I'll see myself home. I made a mistake. You're not worthy of getting to know me."

He ignored me. The door opened, and we stepped back for people to get out. I walked on first, determined to ignore the jackass. It was pretty empty, but I made my way to the other end of the train and sat down by the window. This section of seats all faced forward. I didn't expect him to take the empty seat right next to me. I wasn't sure I wanted him to. I was both angry and sad.

I glanced around. "You sure it's okay to take this seat next to me? You know what? Never mind, I don't want you near me."

"You have no patience. I go where I please. This seat has my name engraved on it. Which means you are in the wrong place."

He did *not* just toss my words back at me. I stared at him again. I wanted to smack him. Dear God, did I want to smack him. He made me so angry. I've never felt like this before. I took a deep breath and let my anger drain. Violence was not the answer with him. I was left with frustration. Frustration that neither of us really knew the other, would never get past the surface, not at this rate. "You're not who I thought you were."

"Who did you think I was? I thought I made myself pretty clear," he said.

"Doesn't matter now." A sense of loss filled me—for what, I wasn't sure.

"Didn't my tats give me away?"

"Lots of people have tattoos. It's considered a work of art among some. Most of it has meaning to the wearer. Doesn't make them hateful people."

He tilted his head. "What did you think this meant?" He pointed to the HH initials at the side of his neck.

I snorted. I'd seen it as a sign. A sign that I needed to get to know this man, but I'd be damned if I told him that. Instead I said, "My initials are HH."

He laughed loud, long and hard.

It took me a minute but I got it. "Heil Hitler." I shook my head at my stupidity because I felt stupid now. Here I was, chasing a dream. The dream of this handsome man, whose mere presence had intrigued me, but he was screwed up, more than most. But, the damn thing was, for whatever reason, I'd been drawn to him, and I found I still was, which seriously pissed me off—that and his laughter.

He finally stopped laughing.

"It's not that funny." But, I felt foolish.

He stared at me without cracking a smile and said, "There's more...all over my body."

It was almost flirtatious the way he said it, but while I tried to process that, I needed to know something else. "Swastika?" I asked.

"A few."

He must have read something on my face when he answered. Maybe because my lip curled up into a sneer when I asked.

"You shouldn't be surprised. I also have a black iron cross on my arm. and an assortment of other things that have meaning to me or that I happen to like."

My heart pounded at all of these revelations. Who the hell was this man I had been foolishly searching for this last few weeks? I must have been out of my flipping mind. Still I fought to understand. The train had gone through several stops now, and we were nearing the transfer point, so I could get home. But, I still had questions for him.

"Why?" I asked. I had to know.

He arched a brow. "Why what—the tattoos? I represent my people."

I shook my head. "All of it. And, why are you here with me now?"

12

DACHS

"You're late." Bruno scowled opening the door.

"Nothing new or unusual in this universe." I shrugged. Pacifying Bruno was not something I was concerned about at that moment.

My thoughts still repeated the conversation I'd had with little Ms. Harper on the train—rewind and playback. Wait, what the hell was I thinking? Her race was below mine; there was no need to remember her or respect her. Yet, I made sure she made it home safely and was actually curious about the 'Weakly,' or was it 'Leakly' people that she claimed was proof against the Prof's arguments. What the hell was that name? I needed to ask the Prof about it.

Wait.

Would that give him the idea that I had been thinking about a lot of things—stuff that did not necessarily fall in line with his teachings. I took a deep breath. Talking to him could go one of two ways: Piss him off because I shouldn't be asking questions or open up a dialogue to answer my questions.

The little card she'd given me was burning a hole in my pocket. We should have parted ways. It was my intention to walk away, but with the way she softly called my name, inviting me to her place, I should have ended our connection there and walked away. But, that wasn't what I did. I get invited into female's homes all the time. Telling a woman 'no' happens to me more often than not. That wasn't what did it either. No, it was the way she thrust the edge of some card into my palm. Her fingers brushed my hand. Tickling my skin and sending currents straight to my cock. I didn't, couldn't look at it until I got in the Uber I'd called after making sure she got home. It contained her personal information. It was dangerous that I found myself interested in what she had to say.

This colored girl could be the death of me—literally. How many times would I tell myself this?

"Where the hell did you end up that you took so long to get here?" Bruno grumbled. "I would have met you outside. I wanted to see—"

I'd texted Bruno back that I was going to be late and would take a car to the meeting. I answered before Bruno could finish. "My driver was an old biddy who smelled like mints and liked to chat." I stopped inside the doorway of the apartment. "Do I need to stay out here or am I coming inside?" I angled my chin toward the room in general. The frustration roiling within me had no roots. I couldn't explain it, and that in itself bothered me.

"Don't be an asshole," Bruno grumbled. "The Prof will be here any minute. He's running late after a work meeting."

I stalked past him to the little side bedroom we converted to the organization office. Most places affiliated with us are rural. More room to train—to grow, but the Professor was clear; he wanted to be in the city, the place where the race war was most likely to start—on the front lines of the gutter-based populous. If our leader had his way, we would ignite the battle. Just like in the *Turner Diaries*. Next to *Mein Kampf*, our bible, the *Turner Diaries* was the roadmap.

"Why does this place smell like mothballs and day old food?" The apartment itself needed to be aired out. The front room was dank and cold. I twisted around and marched to the windows to snatch open the worn curtains. Sunlight poured through the window, cutting a bright swath through the shadows. Bruno's clothes were strewn across the little couch, and stacked takeout containers sat on the coffee table amidst soda cans and beer bottles. Bruno was the embodiment of every white, angry, disenfranchised youth the media found time to talk about daily. We might be part of the downtrodden race, but we didn't have to live like it. "The Prof pays the rent." I flicked a finger at the small tower of plastic containers, and they tumbled over. Moldy old sauces and God knew what splattered across the surface.

"Jesus man! I just cleaned that up." Bruno shoved past me and shoved the dishes back to a stack. "Unlike you, my mama is not here to clean up after me."

I made a fist. It wasn't often I fought with my brothers in anger, but after spending time with that little black girl, I had a lot of unspent energy. Fucking or fighting—it would take too long to visit Becky. I really didn't see any other way to release this stress...I swung and connected with Bruno's jaw.

"Now, why you have to go and bring up my mom?" It was a poor excuse, but the asshole didn't know that. Anything could set any one of us off. Looks like I found my trigger.

Bruno plowed a heavy fist into my belly. Pain blossomed from the spot, petals of hurt unfurling along my ribs. I would not let this bastard get the best of me and breathed through the ache filling my chest. Bruno was a good forty pounds heavier and three inches taller than my six foot two inch frame.

He aimed for my face. "A pretty boy's face should get fucked up every now and then."

I blocked and countered, slamming my knuckles into his

side, then pulling back and ramming them into his chest. Bruno clutched my shoulders as he stumbled back, pulling me down with him. We hit the wall and old framed pictures fell to the floor. Shattered glass spread across the ancient threadbare rug. Grunts escaped us with every blow we traded.

Arms wrapped around mine, yanking me up. With me held back, Bruno took the opportunity to crush his fist into my jaw.

Asshole.

The Prof stepped in between us, getting into Bruno's face. His shoulders shook and a mottled red flush colored the back of his neck above the collar of his shirt.

"What the fuck is this shit?" Professor Stephen B. Sharpe, an educator at the University and founder of NMAWP shifted to the side. "We fight those nigger bastards, the wetbacks currently pouring into our country from South America, the fucking Jews that own the government...We do not, we do not—ever, fight each other!"

Bruno stepped back. "He started it."

That was true, and I wasn't going to deny it. "You talk too damn much." Another truth. In the mood I was in I had no desire to hear the noise coming out of his mouth. Always something, Bruno had no aspirations and being in my friend's presence was just enough to bother me. No matter that it all started with that unusual black girl who invaded my mind.

Prof twisted completely around to get in my face. "What the hell is your problem?"

"I'm feeling rambunctious?" The smart ass in me raised his ugly head. For the first time in a long time I did not want to be here. I needed some alone time and going home wouldn't work. That would just invite my mother to stick her nose in my business too.

The sickening thwack to my face, I expected. Professor

Stephen did not suffer smart alecks lightly. The gun muzzle to my temple was something I didn't see coming.

"This is not the time to play with me. Now, I don't know what's gotten into you, but you are going to get your head on straight. It's coming near the time to bring everything together, and I will not let you or anyone else stand in my way. The permits have been issued for our rally, and I planned some fireworks that will propel our organization onto a national platform." Prof ground out the words through clenched teeth. "You need to decide are you in?" The click of the hammer being pulled back thundered through the room. "Or are you out?"

I stared into my mentor's eyes and knew he meant every word. Death was a shadow in the older man's gaze. When had things become so crazy? Where did all this insanity come from or had it always been there?

I refused to die in some shitty ass apartment with brothers I no longer cared about and was quickly losing respect for. I would do what I had to do to walk out this damn room alive. "I'm in, Prof. How can you ask me a question like that? You make the plans; we handle the execution. You know what it's like when you're gearing up for something big, the energy—a good fight was the way for me to calm things down." I shrugged and ignored the pain. I would be bruised black and blue by tomorrow.

To diffuse the situation, I needed not to care. A year ago, six months ago, hell, a week ago I probably wouldn't have. The black girl with the alluring eyes flashed in my head. Realization was a painful kick in my gut, worse than any punch I would take from one of my brothers. No, this was an epic sin in the eyes of the brotherhood, and admitting it, would see a bullet in my brain sooner rather than later.

I wanted to see her again.

Prof eased the hammer back in place and lowered the

weapon. A sinister smile replaced the scowl on his face. "We got family coming in from Kentucky and Gage has arrived from upstate New York. Ingredients we needed to create one hell of some fireworks will all be here by tomorrow. After all, we have to celebrate our heritage with pride and have one hell of a party."

His words went in one ear and came out the other. This was not good. When had that girl weaved her way into my head? I forced a smile. The people around me needed a response and with my mind wrapped around one thing it was impossible to think about the other. Something about a rally march, planning, that was nothing new.

"Yeah!" Bruno punched the air.

Big grins spread across the faces of my brethren. I shook my head and refocused on what was happening around me. I wouldn't see her again, no matter what I wanted. Worrying about her and the bullshit emotions making me a pussy wasn't something I would worry about.

"Let's do this!" I had no idea what I'd agreed to do. This time my smile was real.

13

HARPER

I entered my condo alone and shut the door. I don't know why I even bothered to invite *him* in, even knowing he'd say 'no' yet hoping for a 'yes.' What the hell was wrong with me? What would I have done if he'd actually come in and Justin came over? He could be back from his trip about now.

Shit!

I moved farther into the room and dropped my jacket on the couch, heading into the kitchen to get myself a bottle of water.

I was still surprised Dachs walked me all the way home, even though he didn't say much, but his eyes never stopped scanning the street—as though he was prepared for trouble. We passed quite a few people, mostly young white hipster males some of them were with women, two were even a mixed race couple holding hands. When I glanced at Dachs his eyes tracked them, but his face was stone cold. Not that he didn't have that whole badass look going all along, but he seemed to ramp it up. He didn't offer any comments on the couples. Perhaps that was progress since he was a white boy walking with a black girl.

He never did answer my question, but he did stick to my

side, not quite touching, but I could feel his closeness. As usual I did most of the talking.

"I'm going to have to find out what was covered in the econ class I missed today."

"Why'd you miss class?"

"My damn car wouldn't start. I had to have it towed, then I couldn't get a ride so I was forced to take the subway."

He snorted. "Hmm. Listen, once you get your car back, stay off the T. No need for you to take the subway, and we will never have to run across each other again."

His major contribution to our conversation for most of the way was him telling me I needed to stay away from him. But, unlike the other times, this time it sounded more like a plea instead of a demand. Perhaps, I'd finally gotten through his thick head.

I CAME to a stop in front of one of the buildings lining the street, he'd stopped as soon as I did.

"I live here," I said indicating the entryway. Would you like to come up?"

He glanced at the building. I knew what he saw. There was no doorman but through the entire front windows you could see into the grand entryway. It was sleek, all chrome and white leather, like you might find in a modern hotel. There was a desk with 24-hour concierge service. Guests were signed in even after they were buzzed in.

His face lost that cold expression, now anger infused it so his skin was a little flushed. "This is the shit Prof talks about. How did you get to live in a place like this? Getting ahead with government funded education and jobs while most white people have to scuffle for the crumbs of supposed equal opportunity."

It was my turn to snap back. "Oh, grow up. Stop acting like a two-year-old having a tantrum." The problem was he was an adult and his kind of tantrums were dangerous and could do some serious damage.

The man still lived with his mother for Christ sake. I'd pulled that much out of him when I'd asked him where he lived earlier. He'd answered me reluctantly.

"No, I don't think so," he said. He stared at me as though he were memorizing my face. "I've got to go." He began to step away from me.

"Wait. Here." I took a chance and quickly took out one of my cards from the pocket of my backpack and held it out to him. This would be a turning point for us. I was done with the back and forth, and the sniping at each other, let's see if there was anything there.

He glanced at it without touching it. "Whatever *that* is I don't want it."

"It's my info, so if you'd like to run into me on purpose or to make sure you don't. Up to you to do whatever you want." My heart paused mid beat, my lungs quit moving as I waited to see what he'd do.

Without another word, he snatched the card from me, turned and walked away. I didn't dare stand there watching him in case he changed his mind. Instead, I went into my building up to my condo. Feeling very satisfied on the one hand, like perhaps we'd made progress. It didn't escape my notice, his last words to me were not to stay away, and he took my contact information. I smiled.

My cell phone rang. It was in my purse where I'd dropped in on the side table, and I went over to it. I checked the caller ID, releasing the breath I'd been holding when I saw Serena's image pop up and not Justin. My thoughts hadn't been on my boyfriend much at all lately. Frankly, I didn't want to talk to him right now, not when my thoughts were taken up with someone else.

"Hey, Lady, missed you today. You up for a movie tonight?" Serena asked.

I'd blown her off a few days ago when she wanted to go shopping. One of her favorite stores was having a big sale, and she wanted to get a few outfits for her paid internship in New York this summer. I really didn't feel like a movie, but I felt guilty about changing my plans on her before. I'd opted to take the train that day, on the off chance of running into Dachs. Just like I knew I'd take it tomorrow. Why couldn't I let this guy go?

"Harper!"

"Oh huh? Sorry, what did you say?"

"Movie? What's up with you? For a while now you've kinda not been yourself. Is something going on between you and Justin?"

"Can't tonight, I've got a paper to write. And no—not exactly. Okay, maybe."

"Harper what's going on? Does this have anything to do with that Nazi?"

I cringed. I couldn't deny her accusation. Dachs was that and, yet...I saw he could be so much more. For all the bull he sprouted, he was also intelligent. I just needed him to use that intelligence when it came to those beliefs he espoused. "I don't know. It's me. I...I think I need to break things off with Justin."

"Get the fuck out of here!"

I hadn't meant to say it out loud, not yet, but knew it's what I'd been thinking about for the last couple of weeks, whenever I thought of Justin. We'd only had sex a couple of times in the last month, and the thought of him touching me, made me shiver— not in pleasure. I tuned back into Serena. "Yes. I don't feel for him what he feels for me. Yeah, I know we might seem perfect, but you've always pointed out we are not. I think it's best I let him know, so we can part as friends before things get too intense between us."

"Good luck with that. I think it's about time, though. But, you know he's not going to go quietly into the night. When he asks, 'why,' what are you going to say? I have a thing for a racist? While I agree you and Justin are not perfect for each other, this other dude isn't either."

That got my back up, true or not, he was more than he seemed. "Dachs is not...well yes, but he's just deliberately ignorant. He doesn't want to know any better."

"Girlfriend, it's not your mission in life to educate the fool."

I paused, thinking about what she said. "I'm not so sure about that. I think it's every rational human being's responsibility to not just sit down and let this crap go unchecked. We don't have to be violent and loud about it, but we can be vocal about it and point out the holes in their ideology."

"Yeah, big enough to drive trucks through," Serena chuckled.

"Exactly. A big ass eighteen wheeler." I knew I'd stumped him when I told him about the Leakeys. I wondered if he'd check it out. All it took was a Wi-Fi or cell service connection and an internet search. "That's part of the problem. These people turn their brains off; they don't think for themselves, let others do it for them and blame everyone else for their personal problems instead of themselves. I plan on waking him up."

"Wow! So you plan on seeing him again?"

I sighed. "Honest to God, I don't know." But, I hoped.

"You're crazy. I can't see you bringing him home to introduce him to your father and his wife. Your father will get his gun out and shoot him where he stands, and he'd have the money and connections to get away with it."

"That's not even funny because it would be true. But, it won't come to that. Besides, I may never see him again. He wanted me to stay away from him. So, there will be no reason for my dad to ever meet him." I didn't bother to let her know I gave him my contact information. I knew she'd not be happy about that at all.

"I think you need to do what that man says and stay away from him. He lives in a whole 'nother world."

My phone beeped, letting me know I had another call. For a split second my heart sped up in anticipation of it being Dachs. But, of course, it wasn't Dachs calling. Justin's image popped up. I got off the phone with Serena and took Justin's call. I invited him over later. I couldn't continue like this, dating one man while thinking about another. Whether Dachs called me or not, Justin and I were done—might as well get it over with.

NONE of this would go well. I was stupid to think it would. The moment I opened the door, Justin walked into the condo and reached for me. I stepped out of his way and asked him to take a seat.

"What's going on?" he asked.

I'd been distant with him for a while now, and he knew it. I remained standing near the sofa not sure quite where to start.

He patted the seat beside him, and I took it. He ran his fingers through his dark hair. "Look, I know I've been working a lot recently, and I've tried to give you space, so you could get your schoolwork done. But, I've got a surprise for you. I thought just the two of us could go away this weekend to reconnect. I got us a room at that little bed and breakfast place by the water in upstate New York you liked."

Wasn't going to happen.

I shook my head. "I'm sorry, Justin but, no. A weekend getaway isn't going to fix things between us. Our relationship should be moving forward. We should be growing closer, but we're not. Instead, if anything, we're at a standstill—a rut. Nothing more will come of us. I want more and so should you. I'm sorry."

He stared at me; his forehead crinkled in disbelief. He got up and paced around the living room. His face was flushed in anger, and at first, his sentences were clipped, like he was checking his words before he spoke, so he wouldn't say anything he'd regret. "But, things are good between us. We are *good* together. We belong together. You—we just need more time."

"Times not going to make any difference. It's over."

Then his tone changed, he let the anger seep through. "I cannot believe this. Where is this coming from?" Justin asked.

I shook my head. We were both standing now facing each other. "I'm sorry. It's nothing to do with you."

"It sure as hell has to do with me, with us, since you're telling me it's over."

"We're not right for each other, Justin—not in the way we should be. And, in truth, I'm swamped right now with school and my upcoming spring internship. I need to concentrate on school and myself right now—then, my new job after graduation. I need to do me right now."

"That's bullshit!" Finally, he stopped pacing and looked at me. "Is there someone else? Are you fucking someone else?"

"What! Hell, no."

"Bitch—"

That was it. Nobody called me by anything other than my name in my damn house. "Get out. Get the hell out of my house and delete my number."

He raised his finger and pointed it at my chest. "That's it, you are fucking some—"

I slapped him across his face and pointed to the door. I was so angry. He looked at me with flared nostrils and clenched his fist.

"Don't even think about it," I growled out. "The first man who hits me is a dead one."

He turned on his two thousand dollar pair of loafers and left, slamming the door on his way out.

I took a deep breath and got out a bottle of wine.

I knew then I'd made the right decision to break up with Justin. After being together for a year, if that's how little he thought of me, then he could go screw himself. There was a reason I never gave him access to my place. A part of me knew I'd withheld a part of myself from him.

We came from a similar background and have a similar lifestyle. We should have been perfect for each other. He thought so, as did others, but I'm not sure I ever did.

An image of vibrant blue eyes flashed across my consciousness. I couldn't be more different from the man behind those eyes. We weren't even on the same planet. Yet, I wasn't letting go. I couldn't. Not until I got my point across to that Neanderthal. Someone had to—might as well be me.

I grabbed some leftover Thai food, heated it up and went to my home office. I powered up my laptop, and instead of opening up my documents folder, out of curiosity, I opened up my social media accounts and did a search of Dachs' name. It was unique enough I only got a few hits. None was the one I searched for. I should have known, if he had social media accounts, he'd have them locked down. Since he now had mine, I wondered if he'd search my pages. My accounts were public. I had nothing to hide. Then again, I didn't put a lot of truly personal information on there or any pictures a future employer might take issue with. But the other reason I opened up my accounts, was to change my relationship status to single. I wondered if there was a way I could tell if anyone trolled my pages.

14

DACHS

The meetings for the parade were long and between that, work, and tech classes it had been over a week since I made it home. Mom was blowing up my phone, and I couldn't get the black girl out of my head. Her nagging was annoying, but once I got past that, just listening to the tinkle in her voice as opposed to the words falling from her lips was nice. She was a know-it-all, someone who only sees the world in black and white. Where as I saw the many layers of gray that created the unfairness that surrounded me and my brothers and sisters.

I leaned on the bar. There were plenty of seats on the train, but I was too restless to sit in one place. For the first time in a week, I was going home to sleep—well, that and to see my mom. We may never see eye to eye, but still, I missed the old woman. Digging into my back pocket, I pulled my cell free. It wasn't to reach out to the woman who birthed me. My fingers hovered over the screen.

I knew how to reach the black girl, Harper, an unusual name. I shook my head. The more I thought about her, the more I wanted to know. Curious, I checked out her social media page.

It was frivolous. Based on face value, she led a rather boring life; there was nothing to reflect her thoughts or values—nothing of substance, just pictures of stupid cats and dogs and internet vomit. That wasn't the young black woman I'd met—all spit and fire.

She is beneath you; that blackie doesn't have the right to wash your clothes.

Sentences scrolled through my mind. Just words to some, but they held some truths, and I spent most of my life believing them. Now, and not sure why, I wanted to feel her beside me, against me, under me. My lids drifted shut. Her image filled my mind. The locks of her hair, were they soft? Was her skin supple? My body flushed at my thoughts. It was a fever. Forbidden fruit, I wanted something that technically I shouldn't have. Shouldn't want. What did Gage call it...Jungle Fever.

A long exhale escaped me. I told her to stay away from me and it had been a while since I found her on the train. Still, if Gage talked—no—the big bastard couldn't have, or I would be dead already. Maybe she finally used that brain in her head and listened to what I was saying. At least she wasn't stupid. I am the dumb one for thinking about a woman—a girl—who was nowhere near ready for me. Was it possible that I missed her? Fuck no, it couldn't be. A snort blew through my lips. Hell, I may not be ready for her. Her ideals weren't mine, but her passion in her beliefs—yeah—that I could relate too. I shifted to accommodate my growing erection and glanced around. I had enough labels attached to me. I didn't need pervert added to the list.

"Long time no see. Your bruises are fading." The soft voice spoken on a seductive whisper. "Dachs."

It wasn't her. When words erupted through her mouth, they were usually combative. Not so, this woman standing next to me...I turned my head.

Becky.

"Hey." I pushed off the pole. "You know how it goes. They'll be gone in another day or so." I skimmed my jaw with my fingers. My stop would be coming up soon. The phone I didn't bother to check, I shoved it back into my front pocket.

"What ya up to tonight?" Becky eased closer to me.

Sleep. Maybe a decent conversation with my parents—an iffy possibility given our different views. I gazed into the bottomless blue eyes of my fuck buddy. Becky wasn't someone I would ever commit to. She was a side piece, and I didn't even have a main woman. The pleasure experienced between her thighs was shared by too many of my brothers.

"I got some business to take care of at home."

"It's been a while. Think you could spare a little time for me? I miss our...*talks*."

I stared at her and studied her features. Becky was pretty, but the toll of hanging with the brotherhood was starting to show. Worry lines were beginning to fan out from the corners of her eyes. Her baby pink lip gloss caked at the corners of her mouth. It was rumored she was once the Prof's favorite, but I never bothered to ask. Whatever they had, their business happened before I joined the organization. No need to think too hard about it; she was still available to comfort, wait, Becky called it 'stress relief'. She fucked whoever wanted to fuck when she felt like fucking. A question struck me that I'd never cared about before.

I had an idea. She was part of the Prof's crew when I joined, but I never inquired about it. "Becky, how old are you?"

"Why?" She cocked her head to the side, and her hair tumbled over her shoulder. Her movements felt practiced.

I never cared who she fucked, but how did it affect her? Sharing her amongst the brothers was cool with me. No harm, no foul. If Becky didn't mind, why should I?

It was that black girl's fault.

I was thinking about things I'd never cared about before. "Just a thought."

"My stop is coming up next. Walk me home."

For the first time, I noticed a sadness in the deep blue depths of her eyes. "Yeah, I'll do that."

The train ground to a stop and the cab jerked, lurching me to the side. Instinctively I held out my arm to steady Becky. She gripped my forearm, her blunt fingertips pressing into my skin. I peered down, there was no shocking difference in our color. No shock of electricity from her touch. Becky was comfortable, but the black girl—Harper—would her touch be soothing or fiery?

"You are always a gentleman." The uptick of the corner of her mouth didn't reach her eyes.

"I did learn a few things from my mama." I moved toward the doors as they slid open.

Becky followed, and we left the station in a comfortable silence, slowly trudging up the sidewalk. Halfway to her house, she quietly spoke. "I'm thirty-six. I actually started out as a student of the Prof's." There was a thread of sadness in her tone.

I glanced down at her. I wasn't expecting that admission. She was older than I believed. "Ever thought of making new friends?" That was the million-dollar question. Had anyone ever shaken her resolve—her commitment to White Pride?

"Why? You and the guys, the Prof, the girls I hang with... there is no need to move outside my circle of friends. You understand me." Becky shrugged.

That was the problem. There was a wider world beyond the city's high rises. What happened if we all went our separate ways? If we were exposed to other choices, would our resolve still revolve around each other? God in heaven, but my headache was growing.

"Are you ready for the parade?" She waved her hands in front of my face.

I didn't realize she'd moved. "I've organized the brothers for the march and have taken care of making sure we have the supplies we need. Bruno is handling the other stuff the Prof wants. I'll be ready on my end."

Becky slid her palm up my arm. "You have never failed the brothers or the brotherhood."

She wrapped her fingers around the back of my neck and went up on her toes. Her face was mere inches from mine. Once upon a time...just a week ago...no a little more than that, I would have leaned in. Now, I wasn't interested. I couldn't even work up enough emotion to care.

She wasn't who I wanted.

I am going to hell.

"Your apartment is right up the street." I didn't want to go any further.

"I got some wine. There are a couple beers in the fridge—a nice shower," she purred before pressing her lips to my jaw. The talcum powder scent of her cheap perfume wafted to my nose.

Yeah, I had more of a hard on thinking about the black girl with the alluring smile.

Harper.

"Another day." It would do no good to cross Becky. If she even had a hint as to what I was thinking, exposing me to the others would be my death sentence. Seems like no matter where I turned, I faced danger around every corner. I would have to make some hard choices soon. Decisions I'm not prepared to make. But, I can't keep questioning my foundation. Soon enough someone would realize my thoughts were taking dangerous paths.

Damn, damn, damn.

She settled back on her feet. Becky's eyes narrowed. "You never turned me down before."

"Changes are coming, like the Prof says. There is no time for any distractions." Would she buy my explanation?

A slow smile lifted the corners of her mouth. "Your dedication is...admirable. Another time, then." She shuffled a few steps back, giving me room.

I twisted on my heels and returned in the direction I came. I pulled my cell free and tapped the screen—her number—Harper's. I'd memorized it. She was a pain in the ass, but right then, I wanted to talk—no, argue with her and remind myself why being around her was a bad idea on many levels. We didn't jive and talking to her would never amount to anything important.

She wasn't important.

Any contact between us was foolish. I stared at the screen and tapped the digits before raising the cell to my ear and listening to the ringtones.

"Hello."

Her voice, the soft sound of a simple word. I pressed the phone harder to my ear.

Yeah, I am pretty much damned.

15

HARPER

When I saw the unknown number show up on my phone, I didn't think much of it. I usually don't answer unknown numbers from out of state; they were always those stupid insurance calls. No matter how many times I blocked the numbers there was always another number the same company would call you from, trying to sell you something you didn't need. But this time, it was a local area code and perhaps that's why I answered it.

"Hello," I said, half expecting it to be another one of those stupid cold calls. Instead, I got silence for a moment and my inhaled air got stuck in my chest as I waited for a reply. I knew, just knew who was on the line.

"*Why?* Why can't I get you out of my head?"

I sat down. A good thing there was a bench right there. My legs really did collapse at the sound of the husky notes of his voice—more like a growl really. I was still on campus, late, working on a project and had been for the last few days, so I'd been driving to school. I'd just been heading to my car. I could admit to myself, now, I'd been waiting for his call and had felt a deep seated disappointment when a week of silence had gone by.

I had been driving to school not just because of the late project, but also, because I didn't want to run into him by chance on the train at all. I wanted him to be the one to reach out to me —to take that deliberate next step. I'd already taken all I would or could. He had to meet me the rest of the way. And, my God, he'd called me. I released the breath trapped in my chest and took in another one before I could find my voice.

"Nothing that you haven't done to me."

"You're not taking the train?"

I smiled. Was he looking for me? And, I asked him, "Why? Did you miss me?" Silence. I chuckled. "Well it took you long enough to call me."

"Were you wanting me to call?"

"I wouldn't have given you my information if I didn't. I hoped you'd use it, and you did."

"Why?"

"No reason. I just did."

"This is a bad idea...I've...I've got to go."

"No! Wait." I didn't beg. It wasn't in my make up, yet I couldn't let him hang up, let him go. I had thought about him. "Meet me. Now. Anywhere, name the place. I have my car. I can even pick you up. We can go somewhere and just...talk." I was rambling but I didn't care, not if it worked. I was supposed to meet my dad for dinner and was running late, but I'd reschedule with him.

He took a long time before answering. "An hour." He spouted off the name of the sports bar just down the street from my condo, then hung up.

It had been awhile since I smiled so much. I got into my car and remembered to text my dad, asking for a rain check. He and his wife were back in town, and he wanted us to have dinner together, like we were a family.

Not.

But, it would be nice to see my dad. Maybe when I rescheduled it, I could do lunch instead, on one of his wife's spa days. That thought cheered me up even more.

Because of the rush hour traffic, it took me a bit longer to get home than usual. But, I had just enough time to change my top, something a little sexier and low cut. My heavy coat will keep me warm. The black leggings and short boots looked great on my legs. I added a little lip cream, took the binding out of my hair and let it flow over one shoulder and down my back to the top of my ass. I smiled at my reflection and rushed out the door.

When I got outside, I took a deep breath and headed for the restaurant. I didn't realize I'd been holding my breath ever since, until I pushed the door open for the sports bar, and the aroma of meat on the grill hit me. It wasn't an especially large place and just down the street from my condo. There were several televisions on all the time, showing one sport or another. I'd been there a couple of times. They made good burgers and only served American beer. It wasn't very pricey but still a very modern, trendy restaurant. The bar was all chrome and glass instead of dark wood.

"May I help you?" the hostess at the front asked.

I'd been scanning the restaurant and at first I didn't spot him, and then, I did. His eyes pinned me like lasers. He sat all the way in the back at the last booth with his back to the wall. "Thanks, I see who I'm here to meet."

I moved past all the tables. The place was full but not crowded, with lots of young people like myself, who either lived or worked in the area, but I didn't recognize anyone.

I slid into the booth, took off my jacket and placed it beside me—all the while, we just stared at each other. We might have done that all night, but the waitress came over and placed a couple of glasses of water in front of us. He must not have been here long if she was just getting the water for him too.

"I'll give you a minute to look over the menu," she said. Two menus already sat on the table. "If you have any questions let me know. Meanwhile, what can I get you from the bar?"

I ordered a glass of Chardonnay, and he ordered beer, then she moved off.

I took off my jacket and settled down, placing my arms on the table, suddenly feeling very self-conscious to be there with him. For the first time, our meeting was very deliberate. Yet, he came when I asked.

Because I asked?

What did that mean?

"Well..." he said, breaking the silence between us. His arms were folded across his chest, and his jacket was still on, not because he was cold, but like he still wasn't sure if he should be there or not.

"Well what?"

"I'm here—talk." His chest inflated as he inhaled.

"I have a question for you, first." I stared at him. Faded bruises outlined in deep purple marred his cheek. "What happened to your face?"

Lord, was he violent? Of course he was.

The waitress took that moment to show up with our drinks.

"It's nothing—a disagreement between brothers." A wisp of a smile lifted the corner of his mouth.

"Ready to order?" the waitress asked.

"Give us a few more minutes," I said, never taking my eyes off Dachs; his hadn't left mine either—like we were both scared if we glanced away the other might disappear. "You have brothers?"

"Not by blood."

I nodded, deciding to forgo the twenty questions. Some guys were like that with each other. The two guys so far I'd seen him with definitely gave off that kind of vibe. I glanced away and looked at the waitress who'd just left us. She was blond, busty and curvy with a cute face. I turned my attention back to him. "She seems more your type," I said.

"You're curious about my type?" A wisp of a smile sent the corners of his mouth up.

I shook my head and took a sip of my wine. "No, not really. You're not my type either."

"Still, you waited for my call. What do you want?"

"Why did you call me?"

He reached for his beer and took a sip. "That was a mistake. I lost my senses for a minute."

"Yet, you're here."

He glanced away from me, looking around before returning his gaze to mine. "I don't know why. Right then, I just wanted to hear your voice."

My stomach muscles fluttered at his words. This is what I'd been waiting for. "Yeah, I get it. Me either—I don't know why I'm here, I mean. But, I know I have been thinking about you. Have you been thinking about me?"

He waved his hand back and forth between us. "This...me, you—we can't be."

His voice was low, laced with anguish. There was a sadness in his eyes, or confusion, perhaps both. But, I had to respond to him. I couldn't help but respond to what I saw in those light irises. "I don't want to sound like a recording, but I repeat: And yet, you called me, and you are here. What does that mean?"

"It means it can never happen again."

That fluttering stopped. I suddenly didn't want to eat. "Are you hungry?"

"Not really," he said.

"Let's get out of here."

"Where are we going?"

"Just for a walk. There's a small park near here."

He frowned. "That's really not a good idea."

Dachs knew as well as I did that some places weren't safe even in the daylight. "It's fine, and it's not that late. It's barely eight."

He called the waitress over and told her we were leaving. She brought the check and he dropped some bills on the table. I stood and walked out. I could feel him stalking behind me. We hit the sidewalk and stared at each other. It was like we couldn't stop, like in spite of who we were as individuals, something connected us really tugged at us. Even the cold in the air showed our breaths curling around each other. I shook my head to clear my fanciful thoughts.

"Something else on your mind?"

"Nothing." I wasn't ready to share that with him yet, if ever. "Come on, this way." I snapped my coat closed. We walked a couple of blocks over to the park. It was part of a residential complex but also open to the public. There was a fountain in the center and benches around it, but it had been turned off. It was all in a very open space. You could be seen from the street. I walked over to one of the benches and sat down. You couldn't see the water from there, but you could see the lights of the buildings. It was a pretty spot and quiet. Even though it was cold out, there was no snow on the ground and for those of us who live here you kind of get used to it. It wasn't so cold we couldn't just sit and talk for a while. Although, what exactly I wanted to say to him, I really wasn't sure. Yet, when he sat beside me, even though he didn't touch me, he sat close enough, I could feel his heat and smell the clean fragrance of him, probably from his soap.

"Did you take a shower before coming to see me?" I asked. I don't know why I did.

Nerves.

I was nervous with him. I could feel my stomach muscles cramp up; they had been tight from the time he'd called me. Just from the anticipation. I shivered. Lord this man could give me an ulcer.

"You cold?"

"No."

He chuckled. "Yeah, I'm clean. If you want to go home…"

I shook my head. "No. Why are you the way you are?"

"I just am. Like you are the way you are. You're trembling."

"Yes, but it's not because I'm cold." I glanced over at him.

"Are you scared of me?"

"No."

I'm not exactly sure which of us moved or leaned toward the other first. But, suddenly our shoulders were touching. He cupped my face with his calloused hand and I placed mine over his. Neither of us were wearing gloves. A jolt seemed to course back and forth between us. There was a connection. His eyes widened; yes, he felt it too. I wasn't alone in whatever this craziness was.

He tilted his head, and I angled mine to meet the touch of his lips. Tentative at first, our eyes were both still open. Then mine drifted shut as he pressed his mouth more firmly against mine. I parted my lips to see what he'd do, and when his tongue touched mine, all thought fled as fire burned through my soul as he consumed me. Neither of our lips were cool any more.

I shifted to lean into him, placing my arms around his neck, one of his hands remained on my face, the other unsnapped my coat and snaked through the opening to grasp my waist, pulling me closer to him. Until we were flush against each other, my leg was angled over his. My shirt rose, and I felt his fingers touch skin. I shivered and could feel liquid pooling between my legs.

It wasn't enough. I wanted more skin against skin. His hand moved just enough to brush against the edge of my bra but not quite touching my breast, which drove me crazy. I moaned into his mouth, and he swallowed the sound. The noise of a car back firing had us both lifting our heads but, my heart continued to race. I was still pressed against Dachs and could feel his heart doing the same. He glanced in the direction of the roadway, then his gaze returned to mine or rather to my mouth. I waited for him to kiss me some more, when he didn't I was just about to take the initiative, but he slowly moved his hand off me, and I released my hold on him. He stood and took my hand, helping me to stand too.

"I'll walk you home."

I was disappointed that he didn't keep kissing me, something had changed. He was thinking again, too much, so I knew he wouldn't come home with me. Still, I knew I'd invite him up. We didn't say a word on the ten minute walk to my front entrance, he stopped and looked at me.

"Come up," I said.

He shook his head. "No. I can't."

"Yes, you can."

"I...I have to go." He stared at my lips and like a flower to sunshine I leaned toward him, but this time he only raised his thumb and traced it over my mouth twice.

"Will you call me again?"

"You have my number now." He turned and walked away.

Smiling, I watched him for a minute, then opened the door.

16

DACHS

I will forever equate the sweet taste of wine to her lips. The feel of her mouth against mine is embedded in my memory.

What the hell was I thinking? Contacting her was a mistake. I should never have touched her.

The party was winding down. A pre-celebration for the success of the White Pride Parade that we would participate in tomorrow. The Prof had kegs of beer delivered; whiskey bottles lined the kitchen counter with large bottles of cola and cartons of juice. Ice-filled coolers lined the floor of the galley kitchen. The crowd had thinned out with couples breaking away to find a quiet corner to themselves—before the true fun began.

I sat in a lone, high back chair by the window, nursing the same bottle of beer I started with an hour ago. Getting drunk, losing my senses, this was getting old. The new members of the brotherhood, youngsters really, one as young as thirteen, were loud and rambunctious. This was their initiation. There was an exuberance to their behavior, a freedom I well understood. As a group, we were invincible and no one, not even our parents, could tell us what to do. Later, when they weren't thinking about it, they would be blooded in. I remember being beaten until my body was so bruised and bloody, it hurt simply to take a breath. It would be no less for the new members, the point of no return.

I sucked in a deep breath and sank farther into the seat, allowing my eyelids to drift shut. It was her eyes, the molten milk chocolate, I got lost in. Before I knew it, I had to touch her. She thought I was scared to go out at night. That was cute; the night was my playtime. I was more concerned with being seen. In that neighborhood, it was unlikely, but if anyone discovered my secret...*her*...shit would roll downhill. I wasn't ready to admit to myself that there was something between me and the girl, *Harper.* How could I explain it to anyone else? Those closest to me would see it as betrayal. Not only would I be killed, but she would too. I couldn't let that happen.

"Something troubling you, son?"

I lifted my lids to stare at the Prof staring down at me. His smile felt forced, and his shoulders looked tense. I took a sip of my beer and collected my thoughts. It was better to keep my thoughts to myself. A corner of my mouth inched up. "Nope, just thinking about the march. Those niggers are in for a rude awakening when they realize that we are running a counter protest to their black parade."

The lines on Prof's face eased. He took a seat on the ottoman. "It will be an event those monkey asses will never see coming." A long sigh escaped my mentor. "I have been worried about you."

"Why?" Had I unknowingly let something slip? This girl, she'd managed to twist my thoughts, and I was too wrapped up in the simple touch of her to think about anything else.

Dammit.

"You're not your usual happy go lucky self. You seem— somber, distant."

"I have a lot of shit on my plate. School, work, this." I waved my index finger in a circle.

"And, a new girlfriend, maybe?" Becky sauntered up to us, a tall glass of dark liquid in her hand.

Shit.

Panic choked me for a moment. Slowly, I lifted my head to meet her gaze. It took everything in me to keep my features neutral.

She winked. "I mean, how else can you resist all of this?" She did a little shake and giggled, falling into the Prof's side. Her beverage sloshed over the rim to splatter on the dingy floor.

Prof caught her around the waist. "Becky, baby, we are discussing business, go play; I'll find you later."

She pouted. "Fine." Then in a singsong tone, "But you owe me." She pushed off his shoulders and ambled away.

"Is that it, you found someone?" Prof cocked his head. "If so, don't hide her, bring the girl into our family. I'd like to meet the young lady that has caught your eye. Knowing you, I bet she is a pure blood beauty."

That will never happen—so many ways that would go epically wrong. Time to change the subject.

"We are celebrating a bit early. Is there a reason?" Usually we partied after a parade. A way to let off steam, from all the emotions that run the gauntlet through us. The anger and combativeness created by people who opposed our voicing our opinions. Seemed the first amendment only counted when it worked in certain people's favor.

"We party tonight and will have another one tomorrow." He shrugged. "Great things are happening. Soon enough, the world will know exactly who we are.

"I haven't seen Bruno tonight." Something was off. Bruno was like our mentor's shadow. His friend ate, shit and breathed the Prof's words, and mimicked his actions.

"He had some last minute ends to tie up." Prof set his beer down between his legs. "Tomorrow is going to be fucking fantastic!" He nodded emphatically, jubilation clear on his features.

"What exactly is Bruno working on?" The get together tonight was one thing, my crazy ass buddy missing it was another. It felt like a half arranged puzzle, and I couldn't quite put my finger on it. He'd never missed a new members' welcome party. "Will he be joining the jump in for the new members?"

"If he can finish the job I gave him on time."

"Why do I feel like there is something you're not telling me?" My mentor liked to keep plans in compartments. It wasn't the first time the Prof was giving each member a specific job, but it was the first time I wasn't part of the main team included in the plan in its entirety.

Prof stilled. He cocked his head to the side. "Are you questioning my authority?"

My cell buzzed in my pocket. I pulled it free and glanced at it.

Harper.

I returned my gaze to the Prof. "I have to take this." I rose out of my seat and worked my way toward the exit. "Yeah."

"Where are you?"

"A party of sorts." Tomorrow was Saturday and parades celebrating Martin Luther King were slated to happen most of the day. It occurred to him—Harper was very vocal. Her beliefs were as strong as his. "Are you going to any parades?" With the inevitable counter protest, things would get dangerous for her.

"I was thinking about it."

"Don't go." I was walking a razor's edge, caught between my life and a woman who was quickly becoming important to me. It had only been a few days since I saw her. I wanted—no need to see her again.

"What's in it for me?" There was a sexy purr to the way she spoke the words.

My dick jerked, and I adjusted it. "I don't want to see you get hurt."

"Why? What's going on…"

The screen door rammed into my shoulder blades. Another member stuck his head through the gap. "Hey Dachs; it's time."

I nodded my acknowledgement. "I gotta go. Don't go anywhere near the parades." My belly roiled. I had a sinking feeling more was planned than the usual fist-fights and verbal confrontations that often happened when the followers of two different ideologies clashed. I ended the call and tucked the cell in my back pocket.

I followed my brother into the house. Furniture was pushed around the perimeter of the room to form a circle. Two lamps cast intersecting circles of light while sending the rest of the room into shadow. Six boys stood in the middle of the room surrounded by bigger men. Some women stood to the side, while others stood with the older members of the brotherhood.

Prof joined the guys standing nervously in the center. Some of them formed fists while others nervously shifted from one foot to the other. Our leader smiled. "Are you ready to join the brotherhood—to accept your place in white society?"

A few nodded, most didn't do anything. Snickers rose up from the group surrounding them. "Speak up!" someone yelled from a dark corner; others laughed.

These were kids; did I look that scared at my induction? Music was turned up and a popular heavy metal song blasted through the room.

Motherfucking Jews need to die! The blood of a nigger is black blood! If you're not white…

"Get the fuck out of the way!" Bruno's voice burst through

the room. He broke through the crowd with his fist raised and slammed it into the closest boy's jaw, yelling, "Blood In!"

We closed in on the new members in a frenzy. I rammed my hand into the soft belly of the bigger teen. To be beaten by your brother was an honor. Music turned to the highest volume poured from speakers someone had set up. Punk lyrics about the superiority of the white man surrounded us, egging us on into more violence. Sweat peppered my face and damped the collar of my shirt from the fight. I threw a few more punches plowing into the eye of some young kid as I made my way toward the kitchen. This was family. I should have been engrossed in showing my new brothers love at the ends of my fists. The grunts, the laughter, the screams of pain and encouragement. None of it felt right anymore. I grabbed a bottle of beer and leaned on the counter watching the 'Blood In.' Tomorrow would be here soon enough, and I would see exactly what Prof and Bruno planned. A sliver of uneasiness slithered down my spine.

17

HARPER

"Wait!" But, all I heard was the dial tone when he hung up. What did he mean by 'he didn't want to see me get hurt?' Why would I get hurt going down to any of the parades? I'd been sitting on my window seat looking out on the traffic below. I called him back to ask him to explain; he couldn't just say something like that and leave it hanging out there.

It went straight into his voicemail. I left him a message, telling him to call me. I didn't bother to send him a text too. I started to, but either he'd call or text. Besides, I was running late. I had to go and meet my dad for our monthly dinner; I couldn't cancel this one.

We always had dinner, just the two of us, at least once a month when he was in town. Even sometimes when he was out of town on business, depending on where he was, he'd come back alone to Boston just to have dinner with me. Then he'd take a redeye back to wherever he had been. After he'd gotten married to his second wife, he'd tried to include her—that lasted once. At the time, I didn't bother to get up and walk out on them. I just glared at her all night. You would think I was too mature for that now but five years ago, the first time he took me to dinner to 'introduce me' to his new fiancée, I did get up and walk out. Imagine my shock when I saw it was our old housekeeper's daughter. I didn't even know they'd been dating. Still, over the years, I made peace of a sort with him. I love my dad and know he loves me too; no one was getting between us, so I gritted my teeth. It helped he travelled so much, and she wasn't always with him, so I never had to see her much. That was the way he tried to keep the peace.

After they were married, the first time she tried to join us for our daddy/daughter dinner, I said not a word. I finished my dinner, declined dessert, said my 'goodnights,' and left. I'd had enough of listening to her talk about how she redid the townhouse and the condo on the beach all by herself. Then, why did I glimpse a bill from a well-known designer for the tune of $100,000 in my dad's office? That was just for the townhouse. 'Did it herself,' my ass. I don't know who she was trying to impress. Then, she had the nerve to want to take me shopping. I don't think so. I'd called my dad the next day and told him, unless he wanted me to fall asleep in the middle of her scintillating conversation, he needed to leave her at home.

He did. But, I had to compromise. In return, I dutifully went home for a couple of hours for Thanksgiving and Christmas dinner. Which, thank God, included a host of friends and my dad's business acquaintances and their wives and adult children. Some of whom I knew, but these were people I could actually have a conversation with that didn't involve the differences in the shades of sunset white and moon white. It's frigging WHITE.

As I called an Uber, my car was acting up again—something I planned on discussing with my father, I checked my phone again—nothing from Dachs. I missed him. I hadn't seen him on the train, and this was the first time I'd tried to call him. I'd have called sooner, but I was busy; I had a paper to finish and hung out with Serena one night. Besides, I wouldn't have been good for his ego if I'd called him the next day. He had enough of that as it was.

"Hi, Dad," I said when I met him at one of our favorite restaurants. Usually, we like to try new restaurants; we both love good food, but we had our favorites. I wanted homemade pasta tonight or 'handmade' since it was served in a restaurant.

He stood and gave me a hug, kissing my cheek. "Hi, honey, you look happy."

I sat down and picked up the menu, although, I pretty much knew it by heart. I thought about his words while I kinda studied the menu. Yeah, I could be happy, I had Dachs' number, we'd kissed, and I hope we'd do that again, perhaps more. But, I'd be really happy if I had a new car, and I told him so—the last thought.

He chuckled. "Well, graduation is coming up."

"I like the color silver." I smiled, leaving it at that.

Dinner with my father was awesome as usual. The only off moment was when he asked me about Justin. I wondered if Justin had said something to him, since he did handle one of my dad's smaller accounts and talked to him from time to time. "We're not seeing each other anymore," I told him.

He seemed surprised. "I'm sorry to hear that. I like him."

"He's an ass."

My dad frowned. "Should I turn over the Tanner account elsewhere?"

I paused. For all the family drama I had in my life, it was mild compared to others. My dad loved me, and if I said 'yes,' he'd do it in a heartbeat, no questions asked. But, I wasn't a petty kind of person. So, I let my dad know I was cool, and the decision was his. "Is he making you money?"

"That's not the point," he responded.

"If you're happy with the job he's doing then it's all good. My relationship with him never had anything to do with you using him to manage your money, and my ending it, shouldn't either. As long as he's not invited to any family or business events I'm attending, it's all good."

My dad nodded and walked me out to wait for a car. As we stood on the sidewalk, he asked the question that had my brain pinging.

"Are you going to any of the parades?"

"I'd been planning on it."

"Just stay away from the protestors. Those people took out a permit to protest too but were only granted access to one area. Just check where that is and stay far away from them. This group seems to sprout a lot of violence."

The more Dad talked, the more my insides twisted. What Dachs said was beginning to make sense.

I drove home in a bit of a daze. The parades were happening tomorrow. My mind kept going back to the fact there were going to be counter protestors—of course, there were. Would *he* be among them? I'd planned on going to watch one of the larger city-planned parades, just to stand on the sidewalk and cheer on the marching bands and floats honoring Dr. King. I'd never considered being anywhere near the assholes who were doing a counter protest. I knew some of my college peers were planning on heckling the counter protestors, Serena being one. I wasn't sure where that would be.

As soon as I got home, I called my friend.

"Hey, Lady, what's up?"

"You still going to a counter parade?"

"Yeah, there's only one, over by that pierogi shop we took you to last month. About a block over from the main one you were going to, I think. Why? You going to come with us?"

I realized that's exactly what I had to do. How could I not?

Yet, Dachs' words sat like a stone in my gut. What would I do if he was among the protestors? What would I do if he was holding hateful signs and shouting bullshit? All on a day that had been set aside to celebrate the accomplishments and achievements of one of the most beloved black men in history. I'd even seen a mural of Martin Luther King, Jr. in celebration of the Civil Rights Movement on the Freedom Wall in Belfast, along with many others. White people in another country celebrate the Civil Rights Movement and its leaders, yet here, we face this bullshit.

"Yes. I'm coming. I'll meet you at your place in the morning."

I set the cell on the nightstand beside the bed and changed into a chemise before climbing under the covers. I loved my king size bed; it was the perfect combo of firm yet soft for me. I wondered if Dachs would like it. I might be getting ahead of myself; he might never get the chance.

The phone rang, and I picked it up, grinning when I saw who it was. Oh yes, there was a distinct possibility.

I settled back against my down pillows and said, "Hello."

18
____

DACHS

It was late. Bare branches danced on the cold breeze. I trudged down the street thinking. I didn't want to go home, but I was in no mood to couch surf at a brother's house either. Actually, I knew exactly whose company I wanted to be in, but that would be dangerous. I stopped and dropped my head back to gaze up. Beyond the trees and buildings, a swath of starless black sky curled around roof tops. There were many nights when I wouldn't—didn't want to deal with my mom, and in trying to prove myself to the brotherhood, refused to bother the Prof. Wouldn't be the first time I slept on a park bench. I learned a long time ago to leave something, clothes, deodorant, any little thing I might need tucked into the corners of the different homes I might sleep in at any given time. If I had to sleep outside, then I would just clean-up wherever I was welcome. Funny, I hadn't thought about my situation, the way I chose to live, in a long time.

I am unsettled, at odds with myself—family troubles, work —the brotherhood and Harper, too many things coming at me at once. A deep, uncomfortable feeling lodged in my chest. I hadn't seen Bruno since the party.

Crisp air blew across my face. I glanced around. The sidewalk was clear. Only partiers and criminals hung out at this time of night. I dug my cell from my pocket and stared at the screen for a while. A simple tap, and I could call her. My finger hovered over the phone for a moment. I pressed my fingertip on the tiny phone icon beside her number and waited.

"Hello."

The sultry tone of her voice sent frissons of awareness along my spine. I needed to make sure she wasn't going to be at the parade tomorrow. That was the only reason I called. Yeah, I would keep telling myself that. "You're not going to the parades tomorrow—right?" I was lying to myself. I wanted to hear Harper's voice.

"I am."

"Don't. I'll be there. My brothers will be there."

"So what?"

She wasn't listening, and I don't know how to make her understand this will not be a normal march. What I do believe is that there will be more than the normal bullshit verbal clashes and fights. "Stay home."

"I don't know how you are going to stop me." Her voice was firm, adamant.

And, we were back to this. The bullshit defiant, I know better than everybody else attitude. I wanted her, and I didn't. Not when she came across as holier than thou, I can do what I want because I can, without a care as to who her choices might hurt... I blew out a long sigh. The mask she wore was as deeply embedded in her as mine was in me. Telling her the truth was all I could do. "I can't protect you." I stopped and inhaled. That was it. Harper had become the woman that I had to keep safe. And, I was willing to put my life on the line to make sure that happened. The influence I allowed her was damned scary.

"What's going on?"

I heard her concern. Explaining the situation, how I wasn't completely sure myself what would happen. There was nothing I could tell her in certainty. She wouldn't accept that, but that was all I could give her. "Something." I shook my head and realized she couldn't see me. "I'm not sure."

"Talk to me."

I wanted more. Not just to see her and hold her, talk to her. But to tell her—everything. "I would if I could." It wasn't a chat we could have over the phone.

"Come to me."

Her voice changed, from questioning concern to sultry enticement. I felt the pull in my gut. My dick jerked in my crotch. "Can't."

"Yes, you can. You are free to choose. As am I. I'll meet you downstairs in my lobby in half an hour." She was quiet for a moment. "I'll see you—shortly."

Silence was left in her wake, she'd disconnected the call. I checked the time before tapping the car app. It was too late to catch the last train. Twenty minutes until I could catch a ride. My decision was made no matter what I told her. I texted Harper.

Give me forty.

Done.

Her message appeared almost immediately.

I increased my pace to make sure I met the car at the corner. While walking I tried again to call Bruno. At the Jump In party, he was there and suddenly, he wasn't. The Prof wasn't giving up shit, so the only way I would probably get any information is by talking to Bruno. The call went straight to voicemail.

"Call me, Brother, We need to coordinate some things." I ended the call and continued up the street.

My cell buzzed. The Uber was closer than I thought. I'd been standing about ten minutes when the car pulled up. Traffic was light, the chimes of my cell filled the automobile's interior. I checked the ID and raised the phone to my ear.

"You looking for Bruno." Prof tight tone bled through the earpiece. "He just called to tell me you're reaching out to him."

"I wanted to make sure we were on the same page with where we are meeting up tomorrow."

"Bruno is still working on the project I gave him. He will be heading a special group of brothers."

"The permits we got have shortened the planned route." Becky had already given me the information since she'd pulled the permits.

"Bruno is aware of where to go, and what needs to happen." Prof's tone brooked no argument.

Too fucking bad.

Something more was going down, and it was necessary to get as much information as possible. I believed in white pride and would support the cause, but fuck if I would suffer for the bull-shit of fucked up planning. Jail time was not an option I was ready to suffer for the fantasies of others.

"What exactly is Bruno doing?" The only way I would get an answer is if I asked the fucking question, directly.

"That is on a need to know basis and frankly my trust in you has eroded."

I already knew that. "I will only do jail time for the right reasons." My faith in the Prof—the brethren was shaken. I needed to make clear exactly where I stood.

"Then do your job and don't get caught. White Power." The call ended in nothingness.

What the fuck did that mean? The driver pulled up to the curb. It was safer that way in case the Prof decided to have me watched. High rises rose up along the streets. I exited the vehi-cle. Harper's building was down the path and just behind the floor to ceiling windows, I could see her pacing near the entrance.

The closer I got to her place the stronger my heartbeat. She looked up and our gazes met. I was lost for a minute in her deep chocolate iris'. The world stopped around me.

She moved, breaking eye contact, and exited through the sliding glass doors. I trotted up to her, catching her around the shoulders and yanking her against me, the softness of her body molding to the angles of mine. She felt so fucking good. I skimmed my palms down her back and curled them around the gentle curve of her ass. I tried to figure out when this black girl had become so damn important to my state of mind. "I missed you." The words slipped out before I realized I'd said them.

She searched my face and smiled. That all knowing smile like she had a secret she was about to share. Without a word, she eased out of my hold and took my hand to lead me through the doors.

I followed willingly, through the lobby, to the elevators, content with my choice to find her...to be with her. Harper pressed the button with the arrow pointing up. Not one word was uttered between us still as we waited. Tension building along my nerves gave my dick life. The doors quietly slid open, and the cab dipped when we stepped over the threshold. She pushed the 20th floor button, and I eased back, watching the shiny metal doors close.

The minute those seams sealed, I wouldn't—-couldn't— deny myself any longer. I leaned forward and wrapped my arms around her waist yanking her back. I dropped my head to her nape. Her scent filled me, wrapping around us as I traced the column of her neck with my tongue. Slipping my hands beneath the elastic waistband of her lounge pants to rest against her flat stomach. Her satin skin filled my palms. She turned in my arms, and I walked her backward. Her body hit the wall with a thud. I curled my hands around her waist and hiked her up to lean on the metal bar attached to the wall, holding my body against hers to keep her in place. Her hair brushed my cheek, and she angled her head. She gripped my jaw in her palms and rammed her lips against mine.

Being gentle was the farthest thing from my mind. There was no going back. I couldn't wait, not anymore. I wouldn't. I broke our connection and reached beside me pressing buttons before I glanced over. The buttons to multiple floors were illuminated except for the one I wanted. I stabbed the red stop button and the cab jerked.

I would fuck Harper now.

19

HARPER

I don't think I realized he'd stopped the elevator until it jerked to a halt. He shifted his hands to my pants and yanked them down. He managed to get one leg out and just ripped the bikini cut underwear I was wearing from the side and everything dropped to pool around my slippered feet. Damned if I cared. As long as he touched me where I ached for him most.

I wrapped my arms around his neck, drawing him back to me. His fingers dug into my hips, his lips returned to mine, and our tongues did this insane tangle—each striving to lead to sate this craving for the other. There was no thought involved, only pure unadulterated emotion, a need to be devoured that ran down to the marrow. He used his larger frame to press his body over mine, pushing my back up against the cool metal wall while his front fully covered me with his heat. His shirt was soft, but the muscles of his chest were hard as they pressed against my breasts making my nipples stiffen. I could feel the roughness of the material of his jeans against my bare pussy. But, I felt even more as he ground his hardness into me. There was zero give, the man was stone hard, but nothing about him was cold—not one bit.

He removed his hand from my hip and brought it around to the front of my body, inserting one finger inside of me. Moving it in as deep as he could go, shifting the angle to do it again and again, placing two of them in there pumping inside me—stretching me. I moved with him, clenching around him, he hooked his finger to find that secret spot. I broke our kiss to take in air on a moan. My body hummed responding to his touch.

"You are so fucking wet."

I would have smiled, but I couldn't. I lowered my arms from around his neck trusting him to hold me in place, since I didn't trust my trembling legs to take any weight if I attempted to stand. I unbuttoned his jeans and touched his zipper.

"Careful," he mumbled before returning to reconnect our mouths.

I was. I had no intentions of damaging what I very much wanted. I pushed his jeans aside enough to free his cock from its confines. It was more than ready to greet me. I ran my hand over as much of him as I could reach. Enjoying the steely silkiness of him, I traced the ridges of his veins pumping the blood into him, keeping him hard. He was longer than expected, so I had to push the jeans aside a little more. I wanted to free all of him, every last delicious inch. His jeans slid down, and he widened his stance, enough that he had room. He squeezed my ass and raised me up a bit higher on the bar so his dick was aligned with my pussy. Dachs broke our kiss.

"Put me inside you, now."

My hand never left his cock. We both glanced down to watch as I joined our bodies. I positioned him right at my opening holding him steady as he jerked forward and upward impaling me onto his hard cock. I sank onto him, seating myself fully on him. We both exhaled in pure pleasure. I closed my eyes; he felt so damn good. My muscles clenched around him, holding him there, forcing us both to be still, to get used to each other and enjoy this moment of our first time. I wanted to remember everything right down to the scent of the soap he'd used to wash with, something masculine and musky. No subtle or fruity fragrance for him. He was all hard male.

I opened my eyes, and he grabbed my thighs. I pushed open his jacket, so I could better wrap my legs around his slim waist. He rocked back before surging forward again. I placed my hands on his shoulders to give myself leverage. Using gravity, he held on to my thighs and pitched upward, while he brought my body downward more fully on him, filling me completely. He did it again and again, slamming his mouth to mine the way he was slamming our bodies together, connecting us.

He switched to slow strokes, he'd pull out almost all the way before rocking back inside me as far as he could reach. Our breathing became irregular, sounding in grunts and pants. I whimpered, as good as he felt inside me I wanted to feel more of him. Where we touched it burned, and I wanted all of my body to feel that. I wish I could have taken his jacket and shirt off. I wanted his skin to cover mine. I wanted his mouth on every part of my body; I wanted to do the same to his.

He must have wanted more too because he used one hand to lift my long sleeved t-shirt up. I wore no bra, and his hand covered my breast. I wasn't especially busty, but he managed to fill his palm with them. He rubbed his thumb back and forth across my nipple, the calluses on his hand creating a friction that had my nipples standing straight up. His rocking motion increased, and I moved with him until he slowed down. I could feel him flexing against my body as he tried to touch as much of me as he could in the space we were in. And God, wherever we touched, he felt good. We felt so damn good together.

He shifted again to take a hold of one leg to raise it a bit higher, and then, he pushed forward. Holding my ass up with both hands now, he really began to move fast and furious. Each surge of his body pressed me farther against the wall, like he wanted my body imprinted on the metal behind me. But each downward glide of my body took him deeper inside me until he was all that there was. We were all that existed. We stopped kissing, his motions were too much, our bodies strained toward each other. I placed my head at the crux of his neck and licked the initials there, cleansing them. My saliva covered them now. They were mine. I tasted the saltiness of skin, wondering if his cum would taste the same, and my body shuddered. Our breathing became haggard, our pace broken as we both tried to take everything from the other, and at once, gave up all that we once were.

At last I felt him give way to the strain in his body as I'd given way once already to mine. He trembled in my arms, and I wanted nothing more than for him to give me what we both so desperately needed.

"Shit!" he called out gruffly.

He actually shook in my arms, his nostrils flared as he fought to inhale, his dick was full but, he hadn't come. He rested on the knife's edge though but fought it. Then it hit me why. He wore no protection.

Holy shit!

I hadn't even thought about it. Everything had happened so fast. My God we were having sex in an elevator. I never lost it like this; I always made my partners use condoms, but he made me wild. From the time I'd first laid eyes on him, all I wanted, needed, was him inside me—right now. But that was stupid. Did he do this all the time? No, no he didn't, and I knew it. "I'm on birth control, and I'm clean," I said and kissed the side of his neck I'd been licking as I contracted my inner muscles.

He groaned. "Jesus! Clean, I mean. I am."

His cock had never softened inside me; it had continued to

pulse against my pussy walls. Unrestrained now, he began to move again, pistoning faster and faster. I could feel his body shudder, giving way to the inevitable between us. He captured my mouth again, sucking on my tongue as his body jerked and cum filled my pussy. The warmth of him inside me triggered my core to react, my inner muscles tightened, and my cum curled around him, mixed with his. I squeezed my thighs against his waist, holding him tightly inside me to ensure I got everything out of him, every last drop. His strokes slowed, and I could feel our joint juices running down my ass cheeks. I couldn't care less. He stopped.

He continued to hold me up while he eased his dick out of me. I lowered my legs from around his waist, but he continued to hold me and made sure I slid down his body. He kissed me hard and pulled away a little as he looked down at himself. His cock no longer stood as stiff as it once had, it was much softer, now, but glistened with the evidence of what we'd just done. Since I was now standing, there was a trail of sticky fluid running down my thigh.

He'd seen it, bent down and ripped off the rest of my under-wear, what little material there was of it, and used it to wipe my leg, inner thighs and between my thighs. Pausing to cup my sex, he dropped to his knees and leaned forward to kiss my shaved pussy. I still had a little juice left in me, and he used his tongue to lick that bit up before pulling up my loungewear. Too bad he didn't stay there long; I was just about to hold his head to keep him there when he got to his feet. He used my underwear to wipe himself off. I got a good look at his cock, now and smiled, even at half mast, the boy was long, veiny and just thick enough. He redid his jeans and stuck my ripped, cum-filled panties into his jacket pocket. I smiled at the mess that made.

"I owe you a pair," he said.

He stared into my eyes with an intensity that had me

searching for breath. Now, I knew what they looked like when he let himself go. There's a beach in Cypress where the water is that shade of blue. "No worries I have more," I said.

"Not from me."

I smiled as he turned around, I couldn't help myself. He released the elevator so it could continue to the other floors. It was lucky that we'd stopped on the 16[th.] floor and he'd pushed the buttons for the floors below and in between, so we didn't have long to go to get to my floor. We were even luckier that it was late, so no one was calling the elevator, and there was a second one available.

He looked at me with that deep gaze again as he rested against the side of the elevator, he raised his hand holding it out to me. I took it, and he drew me to him. I wrapped my arms around his waist, and he kissed my temple, whispering in my ear, "We're not done."

"I sure hope not, but just in case." I kept my head against his chest, so I could listen to his heartbeat and moved one hand to stroke him through his jeans. By the time the elevator got to my floor his heart rate had increased to a nice tempo, and he was hard again.

I only released him once we got to my hallway. There were 8 units on this side of the building, mine was the second corner one off the elevator. I punched in my keycode to let us in. Funny, I knew I would have no trouble giving Dachs my access code. I knew he'd seen me enter it. I'd never allowed Justin to so much as glimpse it. But then, I dismissed him from my mind. He was my past, with Dachs I wanted to look to a future.

I stepped in first and held the door open for him to enter, then shut it. He took a few steps inside and stopped in the entry-way. I tried to see my home through his eyes. I knew exactly what he saw because it was what I wanted my home to say. It was a statement—young, privileged and unapologetic. Why should I be sorry for my father's wealth or the fact I'm well on my way to creating my own. To be fair, my father didn't pay for everything in my condo. Okay, he did buy it for me; it was also an investment, but I did use some of my internship money to furnish the place. Dachs and I could get around to those details later.

My condo was done in varying shades of gray, beige and white. With a few dark colored or black pieces to provide balance—like, my two leather chairs in my reading nook with bay windows that faced the park. I would sit out there and be nice and warm while I read or watched the snowfall. The chairs, one black the other a dark brown, were so soft they could compete with the feel of softened butter and win.

The L shaped dark gray faux suede couch was perfect for entertaining and faced the large flat screen television on the largest wall in the room. The wooden floors were a lighter shade of gray. The cushions, and I had lots of them, were beige with patterns of green or orange hibiscus. There were a couple of knee high vases about a foot at their widest points. One held bamboo sticks twice as high as the vase, and the other held dried branches and eucalyptus branches with the leaves on them just as tall. The vases were the real works of art in the room and not the few pieces of artwork on the wall I'd mostly picked up from craft fairs. I'd picked up one vase in Dubai. I don't dare tell him how much it cost, then how much it cost to have it shipped home to Boston. The other one, I'd at least picked up here in the US. It had been part of an estate sale at Sotheby's. That one cost me a pretty penny too, but they made the living area pop.

He took a couple more steps into the main room; his head turned slightly toward the kitchen, a place I rarely used. Even though I can cook, I actually find it calming, but I just don't have time to do it much. Justin never even knew I could cook. I'd never cooked for him; we'd always get takeout or go out. But I did love my kitchen; it was all white. Everything in there was white in varying shades and textures accented with silver trays. Even the floor was a very ash-gray color that was almost white.

Dachs turned to me; there was a look in his eyes, I couldn't quite place but didn't much like.

I went up to him and placed my arms around him, staring into his face until he stopped looking around and looked only at me, so I knew I had his complete attention.

"Remember what I said about 'choices.' I choose you, and I get what I want and you are what I want. I don't need you to give me anything other than yourself. That's all I need or want. Can you do that? Do you want me?"

20

DACHS

Muted light flooded the bedroom. I woke with a start, my lids snapping open. I lifted my head to search my unrecognizable surroundings. I angled my head up to find Harper sprawled across my chest. Memories slowly flooded my mind, and I settled down, dropping my head back on the pillow. Gently, I skimmed my palm along her back and rested my hand on her bare shoulder. I needed to move, get to the meeting place and try and figure out exactly what the Prof was up to, but I didn't want to. Harper's naked body lay flush against mine, my cock instantly came to life.

There was no time for that—tonight maybe—but not right now. Still, I didn't want to wake her either. I eased my arm beneath my head and stared at the ceiling, enjoying the weight of her on me. If only we could lay like this through the morning.

I was still caught in a cyclone of reflection. Last night, I crossed so many damn lines that there was no going back. I couldn't return to the person I was, but I didn't see a way to move forward either. Not until I clarified exactly where the Prof was leading me, my brothers and sisters. At the end of the day someone had to be responsible. The Prof was acting mysteriously, Bruno had disappeared. Although Gage was part of the brotherhood, each group worked independently, so he had no real say in the Boston chapter and Becky was flighty as shit. There was no one to rely on but myself. Lying here meant I was complacent with whatever hair brained scheme my friends had come up with. The sooner I got the parade protest over with, the quicker I could come back to Harper.

I eased to the side, moving from under her. She grumbled and shifted, turning to the side and curled her body around a pillow. I peered at the way the slim line of her back perfectly dipped into her waist before rising into the gentle curve of her hip. Sheets draped over her legs stopped my perusal. She was black, but I couldn't regret what happened. The thump of my heart sped up. The magic between us—I looked forward to it happening again—after I took care of my business. I glanced around the room; in the stark brightness of day, her wealth couldn't be denied. There were signs of money everywhere from the furniture to the paintings and photographs on the wall. And me, I lived with my parents on a good day and was homeless most other times. I dropped my head;, that never bothered me before. I stood and searched around for my clothes. My shirt and jeans were beside the bed while my jacket was in the living room across the back of the couch. One boot was in the kitchen and the other by the door. I had no idea where my underwear was and didn't have any more time to look for it. With my shirt still open I left Harper's place and solidly shut the door behind me. I paused. Last night, she didn't bother to hide her code to the door; was she trying to tell me something? I shook my head. We weren't that deep into anything, yet. I was probably imagining things.

A bright, sunny day greeted me as I exited the building; the air was a bit cooler than last night, still on the warm side for this time of year. I dug my cell out of my pocket and checked the time. I wanted to send Harper a message. Thirty-eight percent battery.

Shit.

It was easier to leave her sleeping. If she had questions or even asked me to stay, I would have a hard time explaining something I wasn't sure of or denying her request if it meant sliding into her body again. I tapped a quick message into my phone.

Parade not safe – C U 8ter.

Now, I had to find out what was really happening. Chimes drifted from my pocket as I made my way down the street. I pulled my cell from my pocket expecting to see Harper's name flash across the screen. It wasn't who I thought it was.

"Mom."

"Good morning." Her sing song tone wafted through the earpiece. "Do you plan on coming home or should I pack up your things and have your father bring them to you?"

Not once did my mom raise her voice, in no way did she sound angry, but I knew. I heard it in the clipped words she used. My mother was pissed. It wasn't the first time we had this conversation. It had become a weekly ritual. "I'll be home this evening."

"You will come home this morning." She paused. "Part of the parade route will march directly in front of the shop. A lot of people will be in the streets, which means we will be busy. You need to be here to help."

"I have other plans." If I told her I was marching in a counter protest that would just escalate the fight we are going to have. Since I will not be coming to the shop anytime today. I couldn't tell her I'll actually be walking right past it.

She was quiet for a long time. I glanced at the screen to make sure our call was still connected. "What changed? You were such a happy child," she spoke quietly.

Here we go.

"I grew up." It was the only answer I could give her. Things change, I changed. I met a man who opened my eyes to the unfairness in the world. There were a million reasons why and each one of them would give my mother reason to argue with me. "You and Dad are getting older. I told you to hire someone." She never listens to me.

"Why? Why when I have a perfectly good, if foolish, son to do the work."

Deep chuckles escaped me before I realized I was laughing. Mom never did hold anything back. Since meeting Harper, I found myself contemplating everything.

"I have missed your laughter, Dachs. Help me and your father out. Come home, Son." Her voice grew gentle.

Another day, I would have ignored my mother's request and not given it a second thought. Today, I couldn't. There were some urgent things I had to look into but...that hyper awareness couldn't be brushed off. The idea that something was seriously wrong sat like a boulder in my stomach. I would take care of whatever was going down and tomorrow, I could start over. I will go home and talk to my mom. Maybe introduce Harper to my parents. No—it was way too soon for that. What was strange, I really wanted the two women to meet. Fuck there was something wrong with me. "I really have something to do today..." I took a deep breath and exhaled. "I'll help out in the shop tomorrow—all day. You have my word." If I didn't learn anything else from my parents I did pick up if you weren't a man of your word, then you weren't worth shit.

The line was quiet again. I waited.

"I don't think I ever had the chance to tell you—I don't always agree with you, but I am proud of you. You are a man of your own mind. I love you so much."

This is new. I didn't know what to say. I opened my mouth

and strangled to get the words out. To tell her I love her too, but there was nothingness. I pulled the cell from my ear and looked down at a blank screen. The fucking phone finally died. I crossed the street. Another two blocks, and I would be at the T station.

I would meet with my brothers, and we would march. Afterward, I wouldn't stay to celebrate our protest victory. The urge to see my folks was sudden and immense. I needed them to know I loved them too. I stuffed the phone in my pocket and quickened my pace. Movement picked up around me. People getting on with their day. The closer I got to the station the more crowded the sidewalks. Later, I would talk to Mom and Dad. If not tonight, there was always tomorrow.

I trotted down the station stairs two at a time and pulled my wallet from my back pocket for the pass, pressing it against the turnstile as I moved. I am probably overthinking things; Bruno would be at our meeting place, and the Prof's big secret wouldn't be more than bringing in extra soldiers for this race war he was perpetuating. Like every other plan the Prof tried over the years it would most likely fail too. Things would get ugly, the police will intervene, emotions will run high, but no one will go to jail, and better yet, no one will get hurt.

Even I knew it was bullshit I was creating in my head. At least Harper wouldn't be there when everything went to hell.

21

HARPER

The ding of my phone on my nightstand told me I had a text. I stretched my hand out the way I'd done a few times during the night, expecting to touch hard, toned flesh. Instead, I skimmed soft warm sheets. I opened my eyes, and as soon as I did, I knew he was gone. I was a little sad not waking up with him beside me. My plan was to spend the day in bed, exploring each other more, to hell with any parade as long as we spent time together. Last night was incredible. I rubbed my legs against each other, remembering the feel of Dachs legs on mine, mine on his, his tongue on me. I smiled as my body clenched in anticipation. What happened between us was explosive, and oh so good, as I knew it would be.

Then, why did he leave?

I reached for my phone to find out what was going on, when I noticed the text was from Dachs. The smile on my face died when I read his message. "What the hell?" I sat up, suddenly the feeling in my stomach was no longer one of elation but dread. What was going on?

I'd meant to talk to him about what he'd said about staying away from the parade but got sidetracked. Was there real danger involved? After what happened in Charlottesville, no one wanted a repeat of that. With all the precautions I knew the city would take, what else other than a few fights, if that, might happen. Did Dachs know about anything more than that? He already told me he'd be there. If he was going, then so was I. I didn't bother to respond to his text. I'd find out for myself what was happening soon enough. I called Serena to tell her I'd meet her for breakfast then go with them to the parade.

I stepped on the elevator and smiled, remembering last night. The elevator doors closed then came to a stop on the twenty-third floor. I looked up only then, realizing I got on an elevator going up not down. I also noticed something else, the camera.

"Oh shit!"

"Sorry, did you say something?" The person who'd just got on asked.

"Ah no...sorry. I thought I was going down, not up."

I knew what I would have to do. I got off on my floor again and went back to my apartment. I grabbed some spare cash out of my office and got back on the elevator. I would have to bribe someone to forget about that video feed—better yet, delete it.

Instead of going down to my garage for my car, I went to the lobby and stopped at the concierge desk. I breathed a sigh of relief; Pauline was still there. She'd been working last night. She was really sweet, and I knew her, and was always nice to her. I had even given her a ride home once. As soon as she saw me, she had a huge grin on her face. And, I knew she'd seen the video in the elevator.

"Working a double?" I asked.

"Yeah, thought I might be seeing you this morning."

I didn't bother to ditter around. "What will it cost me to have you delete that footage?"

She smiled. Turned to the computer and did something.

"Done! I've done one or two things in my 60 years, I wouldn't want recorded either."

I grinned. "I bet. Wait! What about the cloud?"

"Took care of that too."

I put my hand to my chest. "Thank you. I really appreciate it." I took out the envelope of money I'd planned on bribing whoever was at the desk with to delete that video and handed it to her.

She held up her hand, not taking the envelope. "Oh no, hon. It's fine. I'm just glad it was me here and not Albert."

"Me too. He'd already have it up on YouTube."

She chuckled. "That's true. But tell me one thing, is this your new man?"

I nodded.

"He's my kind of man. Good thing I'm not 20 years younger."

We both laughed, and I took her hand and placed the envelope in it. "Take it—a belated Christmas present." I walked out before she could protest.

I pulled out of my garage feeling much better at least about the sex tape I'd inadvertently made, but the feeling of butterflies going crazy in my stomach over what would happen at the parade today didn't stop. But I had to go.

AFTER BREAKFAST, I left my car at Serena's. We ended up having to take the T. There were hundreds of people everywhere and a lot of streets were blocked off. I think there might have been more people, black and white, lining the sidewalks counter protesting the protestors than were actually watching the official parade a block over.

There is usually a crowd that shows up for the parades, but because there wasn't four feet of snow, which would cancel it or icy cold winds, which would bring out fewer folk, instead, it was unseasonably warm at 60 degrees; there was a hell of a crowd. Most on the sidewalk held signs, with slogans like '*Love Not Hate,*' '*Black Lives Matter,*' and '*Go Hang Yourselves.*' There were many others along the same lines. I stood with Serena and several other Harvard students we'd ridden the T with. We'd gotten there early, but there were already people lining the edge of the sidewalk, and even more arriving, until the sidewalk became four or five people deep for blocks. I found myself elbowed and shoved as people tried to position themselves, but I managed to stay just behind Serena.

Cops lined the street in each direction I could see. Trying to keep those of us on the sidewalk from running into the streets and doing anything to the White Nationalists. I was sure there was some waiting to do that. As the shouting farther down the street got louder, I could feel the tension in the crowd growing. The Nationalists would soon come into our view as they marched up the street toward where we stood.

I glanced at the police in front of us. The presence of that many cops did not reassure me; instead, it had my anxiety levels spiked dangerously high.

Are they really needed?

Of course they were, but who were they there to protect exactly—the crowd from getting out of hand or the counter-protestors antagonizing them?

We heard the chanting, then more shouts from the crowded sidewalks, closer now. It all seemed surreal. Since I wasn't at the front of the crowd, in truth, I couldn't really see all that much. There were at least two taller people in front of me. Serena and I stood more in the middle of the group on the sidewalk. Then, just before the front line of the marchers reached our spot, someone broke from the crowd and got past the police and confronted the young men carrying a flag. They all wore white shirts, with red suspenders, khaki pants and black ties. Even their black Doc. Martens had red shoelaces. The three young white males couldn't have been more than eighteen, if that, carried a flag depicting an iron cross. A black guy with dreads down his back got right in the guy in the center's face. He screamed at them, as did the rest of the crowd along with Serena and my friends. I said not a word not liking any of this. Then the man yanked the flag out of their hands; before anyone could stop him he set it on fire. Turning, he ran into the crowd.

People moved out of his way and tried to block the nearest cops racing after him. Meanwhile, others in the crowd took that as some kind of cue to surge forward as though emboldened by the act of violence. The boys picked up the flag and tried to beat out the fire, but the men behind them just kept marching. It wasn't until a couple of people in front of me stepped aside, that I saw two people I never thought in my life I'd see in the front of this shit show. One was a shock, the other I'd expected.

He told me he'd be there. But still, to see him hurt my heart. A few hours ago, we'd lain together. We'd been as close as two people could physically be.

Dachs.

Dachs marched next to one of my fucking former professors, brandishing hate.

My eyes welled with tears. I was so hurt and angry no words left my mouth. What was there to say? Dachs stared right at me in shock, but neither of us could look away. I could see nothing else but his face and hear nothing else but the breaking of my heart. A tear rolled down my face. The crowd shifted, separating us. But before they did, I read panic in his eyes.

No!

He didn't get to panic. I took a step toward the front, so I could see him again. Just as the world exploded into unrelenting, mind numbing sounds, and I was drawn down into an abyss of hell. Someone shoved me, and I fell to the ground, but one of my friends was there to help me up.

"You okay? We need to get the hell out of here," she said.

"I'm fine." My palms were scratched on the rough sidewalk, but I was otherwise unhurt, I managed to get to my feet.

Pandemonium broke loose. I heard the explosions, then the screaming. It took me a moment to register what was going on. I smelled the fire before I saw a store in flames, then there was another flaming bottle flying toward the people on the sidewalk. Someone was tossing firebombs or something into the crowd. The air filled with smoke, panic and fear—mine included. I'd been so intent on trying to catch Dachs eyes again, wanting to make sure, I don't know what I wanted to do, confront him. But, we had to get out of here. I heard someone, I think Steve, scream, "Serena!"

I turned back around and saw my best friend on the ground, our friends near her. I thought I'd been afraid when I fell. My heart slammed against my chest in true fear now. I made my way over to her, Steve and James knelt beside her, protecting her from getting trampled. We picked her up, but she was unconscious. James held her while I shoved a path through the crowd for us. People were running, some toward the protestors to fight, others away from whatever the hell they were tossing into the crowd. We just needed to get the hell out of there; Serena needed help. I prayed to God she was all right.

22

DACHS

Hell.

I don't understand how I got here, but there was no denying the reality of it.

There was no tomorrow. You can't think about that yet. Mom is alive.

That thought chased itself in my head. My mind kept flipping to what happened, and what was currently going on. This bullshit—my mentor's great plan.

I stopped pacing the hall and leaned my forehead on the cool windowpane. I closed my eyes to block out the images. Instead. different, more vivid pictures ran like a movie through my mind in slow motion. This shouldn't have happened. It wasn't part of the plan. At least not the one I was a part of—the one I helped form.

Beeps and dings echoed faintly through the halls. The low din of chatter from doctors, nurses, patients and visitors almost drowned out the whir of machinery. I lifted my lids and spun around to drop into a chair. A medicinal scent combined with the strong smell of disinfectants created an odor that made me nauseous. I leaned forward and rested my head against my fists.

Slowly I banged my knuckles into my head, harder and harder. Upon arrival to the hospital my mother had been immediately rushed into surgery.

What started out as the usual bullshit I'd done a hundred times over the years, twisted into something unimaginable. Things had gone too far. When two conflicting, highly volatile groups clashed there was bound to be violence. Pepper spray, I was prepared for; Molotov cocktails, I was not.

At some point during the march, when counter protestors acted, it was like my brothers had been given an okay. I sucked in a deep breath and choked on the myriad of odors that got locked in my lungs. Bricks were thrown, that was no surprise. The bottles though, they'd been weaponized. This wasn't some simple thing; it wasn't anything that Prof, Bruno or even Becky had discussed with me. I paused. Did Becky know about this bullshit? This was premeditated.

Gasoline would eat through regular fucking plastic, glass had to be collected. The chats from the night before spiraled through my head.

A special project for Bruno.

My brother had disappeared for weeks prior to the event. The scope of this shit crossed the line into domestic terrorism, and I would be an idiot to think the actions of my group wouldn't have consequences. Stupidity did not excuse a jail sentence—one that could see me behind bars for the remainder of my natural life.

Now, my mother was caught up in this—this hell—I have no clue what else to call it. I rubbed my temple. An errant bottle burst through my family's storefront glass pane and exploded in the shop. Flames erupted near my mom—so close, her clothing caught fire. I exhaled and lifted my head to gaze at my father. My dad sat in a corner, staring out into nothingness. The old man didn't utter a word, rubbing his bandaged hands against each other. In the breath of time my mother was rushed to the hospital, I watched my dad age before my eyes.

I glanced around. Those so-called brothers had scattered after creating chaos. The last person I saw was Bruno running for an alleyway behind the burning pierogi shop. Only God knew where anyone was.

Harper.

She was there, but I got caught up trying to get to my mom. I hadn't bothered to check on her. All I could do was hope she was alright.

If I took a deep breath, I could still smell the ripeness of gasoline on the breeze—feel the heat of multiple fires erupting along the sidewalk beside me as I ran for my home. In the chaos I lost track of Harper.

Jesus, I told her not to come.

I failed both women.

My mom was surrounded by good Samaritans who had taken off shirts and jackets to cover the woman who birthed me. The bit of skin I did see was grotesquely darkened, highlighted by streaks of blood. My dad followed close behind her, his palms raw and bloody. He'd tried to put out the flames consuming my mom with his bare hands. I heard the wails of my father calling my mother's name as he was dragged through the burned out opening of their pierogi shop. An underlying scent of cooking meat wafted to my nose as I burst through the group of observers, and I wasn't sure if it was a vendor, or...I didn't want to think about it. The last image I had of my parents was them being rushed into the ambulance, and the vehicle trying to drive through a crowd that wasn't moving fast enough. I ran behind that ambulance, pushing through people for as long and as far as I could—praying. In a matter of moments, I had become a hypocrite. Even at my lowest, I never asked God for a damn thing, and now, I was begging him—

pleading with whatever greater being would listen to save my mother.

I couldn't watch my dad anymore. How did I tell the man, I looked almost exactly alike, everything was my fault. His wife, my mother, was dying because of the family I'd adopted—men and women, I claimed as brothers and sisters. I glanced up and down the hall. Police would probably be here soon. A coward was not someone I was raised to be. I would own up to my part in the bullshit scheme to my father. I moved to sit beside my dad but glimpsed the Prof marching down the hall, a small entourage in tow. Their faces were stone masks of impassiveness. There were a couple of guys I didn't know—one I did.

Gage.

Did he know what the Prof was up to? Were the men with him, and them, from Gage's chapter, cause I saw no one familiar from ours. A current of uncomfortableness—no—*hate* crackled down my spine,

Prof stopped inches away from me, standing with his feet together, his back straight and head forward. Looking at him, most folks thought he might have served in the military. The S.O.B claimed he couldn't even register because of his flat feet. Fucking bastard took a few steps, invading my personal space. It was an intimidation tactic I'd seen him use before with the new members.

"I came as soon as I heard your mother was attacked." His voice cracked, but I knew it was an act—as if the man I viewed as a friend and mentor, a fucking father figure, didn't instigate everything. "You planned this." Anger roiled, choking me.

"Son, I came to support you. It's those damn people; the ones that don't look like us. They started it! They are framing us! You saw it, they came for us, first. Of course, we are supposed to look bad. Think about what that nigger did not too long ago, paying someone to beat him up and blaming us. It's the same thing. It was another nigger that attacked us first. They can't be trusted." Prof gripped me by the shoulders. His blunt fingertips pressed deep indentations into the fabric covering my skin. Anger choked me, this fucker had the nerve to touch me.

Me!

We were once friends; I bit the inside of my cheek to contain the rage threatening to erupt in me. This is not the place or time to beat his ass. I allowed him to keep talking. "None of those darkies can, and that's what you need to tell the police when they come. That *they* did this and are responsible."

There it was. I lowered my head, not in submission but because I could no longer stomach the sight of him. "I don't have time for this." I stepped away, reminding myself that fighting in the hospital would only add to my troubles.

Prof held tight, squeezing my shoulders, harder.

"You have done enough to my family." My dad was suddenly standing next to us, his face unreadable. "Let my son go." He curled a meaty bandaged-wrapped fist around the Prof's wrist. Dad showed no sign of pain as he gazed at the Prof through clear eyes. "Dachs is my only child, and I will kill you to save him."

The grimace on my mentor's face—I never thought I would see that. I found no pleasure in his true nature being revealed—more so embarrassment. I'd once reveled in his line of shit. My dad, for the first time in my life, I saw him as a hero. He was always the quiet one, between him and my mom. My father is the force behind my mother that enforced her rules.

Surgical staff and doctors filled the little alcove and broke the tension. My dad and I twisted in unison to face them. Beyond them, down the hallway, a familiar woman rounded the corner and hesitated in her steps. I narrowed my eyes—*Harper?* The doctor began speaking, I refocused on the man in the white coat, but what he was saying didn't make sense.

"No!" My father screamed, falling to his knees. The woman he'd been married to for almost thirty years was gone.

I snapped my head back. I didn't hear right. "No, she was fine earlier...I talked—I talked—this morning—" I was repeating the same words over and over again. The doctor was wrong.

"I'm sorry. The burns were substantial, covering over sixty percent of her body. Her heart stopped on the table—several times. There was nothing further we could do." The damn doctor speaking droned on.

Everything in me crumbled. We never had a chance to reconcile. I was going to spend the day with her tomorrow, to sit down and talk without yelling at each other. I peered past the group surrounding me, looking for one person—the woman that had grown so important so quickly to me. God, I needed her.

Harper.

She was there a moment ago; I was sure of it. What was she doing here? Was she hurt? People around me were closing in, suffocating me.

I shoved my way through the group and sprinted down the passage. Slipping around the corner, I met a dead end. There was no one in the short hall. Only a window and an exit with a small sign beside the door denoting steps. I slammed into the bar that released the locking mechanism and the heavy metal barrier swung open. Antiseptic, white-painted flights of steps led up and down, away from the landing. Flood lights above the door illuminated the area.

Harper was halfway down the flight of stairs and moving fast. I charged after her taking the stairs two at a time. She was on the next landing down before I caught up with her. I grabbed her by the elbow and spun her around.

Tiny red dots splattered her shirt. Faint gray streaks marred her cheeks. I curled my hands around her face, tilting it from left to right, searching for the source of the red specks. Blood splatter. Was it hers? "Are you alright?"

"What did you do?" she whispered.

Do? Me? Hell, my mom was gone. I had only ever tried to figure out what the hell everyone was up to.

Harper touched gentle fingers to the place just below my eyes. "You've been crying."

I eased her fingers away to pat my cheek. I didn't realize that tears had flowed. My head hurt and the pressure, as if my brain was about to explode. Nothing, no words came to mind. How could I explain the train wreck going on in my head? I was running on pure emotion. I yanked Harper closer. I needed a reality check to make sure I wasn't dreaming. Her lips were so close, and her eyes were wide.

I crushed her lips under mine and slid my tongue along the seam of her mouth. *Open for me*, I willed in my mind. With the slightest gap I pressed my tongue forward past her teeth, licking at the inside of her cheek. Slowly, I walked her back, devouring her mouth, sucking her lips between my teeth as we moved. A hollow *thud*, and we could move no farther. I pushed my body into hers, shoving my leg between her thighs. Fabric from my shirt bunched in her fists at my sides. A myriad of scents drifted to my nose. Her perfume, sweat, food...*shit,* she could have been killed—died a miserable death like my mother. It wasn't too late. I had to protect her. I cocked my head to the side and rammed my body harder against hers. Her heartbeat thudded against my chest, or maybe it was mine, reaffirming my—*our* survival.

Harper is my shelter in my totally fucked up world. It was selfish, but I wasn't giving her up. There was nothing I wouldn't do to make sure she survived the hell I had descended into. "What happened...I had nothing to do with." I broke our kiss and whispered. But, I would get to the bottom of the bullshit. Those that killed my mother would pay. One way or another.

23

HARPER

I should hate him.

Serena could have been killed by the explosions. It was all so chaotic and like a scene from an apocalyptic movie, except this was no movie set. I will not soon forget the sounds of people screaming or the suffocating smell of smoke in the air. I could still smell it on my clothes. I'm still not exactly sure what happened. One minute I was staring at Dachs, then all hell broke loose. Someone knocked me to the ground, and that might have actually saved me from the flying debris.

But not Serena—thank God, at least her wounds were all superficial, mostly from flying glass, and she suffered a mild concussion when she'd fallen. We were lucky, our entire group was okay, but others were seriously hurt. The emergency room had been crowded. I'd heard the nurses talking about a woman in critical condition. And all because of a bunch of shit for brains.

Dachs.

My heart caught in my throat when I remembered seeing him with those thugs. Was he hurt in the blast? Why should I care? In all the confusion, I lost sight of him and when I saw all the blood on Serena's face, I panicked. I knew we had to get her help. Did *he* have something to do with those bombs, my friend, and all those people getting hurt? My heart stuttered—after last night, everything we were becoming...

No. Please God, no.

"Hey, you okay?"

I came out of my fog and smiled at Serena. There was a large bandage over her eye; she might have a scar on her eyebrow. From all the blood, we thought it was her eye; thank Christ it wasn't. She had a few cuts on her neck but nothing that would scar. "Yeah, yeah, sorry. I'm fine. I think I need to get a soda or something. I need something to wake me up. Do you want one?"

"I'm good."

The nurse came over to tell Serena once her folks got there, she'd be released to go home; she shouldn't be alone for the next twenty-four hours. I'd called her parents as soon as Serena had been placed in the ambulance.

"Their flight already landed; they should be here soon," Serena told her. "I hope James' hands will be okay."

James had come with us to the hospital; he'd suffered from cuts too from the glass blasting onto the sidewalk. He'd raised his hands to protect himself. I hadn't even realized his hand had been cut up. His dad had showed up and had just taken him home. Steven had gone with them.

"He'll be fine. You both will."

"You're right," she smiled.

I gave Serena a hug. We both knew this could have been much worse.

"Where can I find a vending machine?" I asked the nurse.

"The one on this floor is broken, so two floors up."

"I'll be right back."

Just my frigging luck the beverage machines were two floors above. Imagine my shock when I got off the elevator and saw those skinhead assholes standing around, right near the vending machines. Worse, I spied Dachs. He had a jacket on, but he was still dressed like the rest of them. I turned to get back on the elevator, but it was already heading up. I wasn't about to wait for the next one in case he saw me. I turned and headed for the stairwell. I'd only made it down one flight when I heard the door above me slam shut. I didn't bother to look up. I already knew who was behind me. I heard his footfalls pounding down the stairs. Crap, it sounded like he was leaping over a few of them. I wasn't going to break my neck to get away from him, but I didn't stop either.

I'd just reached Serena's floor when my arm was grabbed, and he spun me into him. Even my voice sounded pathetic when I spoke to him. "What did you do?" I had to say it twice. When he told me he had nothing to do with what happened, why do I believe him?

What madness was this that I didn't immediately push this man away—or slap him. Instead, when he drew me to him, I went. I did more than that, I melted into him. Perhaps it was the raw need and pain I saw within the depths of his icy blue eyes or the tracks of tears. Lord, the tears still hovering on his eyelashes were my undoing.

For the span of time we remained in that stairwell—was it two minutes or two lifetimes—it was not enough. He devoured me with his mouth as if I was the only thing anchoring him to this life. I felt every part of him as he walked me backward until he had me up against the wall. I enfolded my arms around him and drew him closer. I needed to be closer to him.

I wrapped one leg around his muscular thigh. He grabbed my leg and raised it higher, pulling it up around his waist. Without releasing his lips from mine, he pressed me against the wall using his body to pin me there. At the same time, he took my other leg and placed that too around his waist. We settled into our own little world with my back pressed against the cool wall, and his heat resting at my front. Just as we had been in the elevator. Just as we had been only last night. I moaned, unable to think straight from the emotions clouding my mind. So much heat I thought I would go up in flames if I didn't have him inside of me. He pressed that hard body into me, and I think we both moaned. A door slammed somewhere, echoing through the stairwell, bringing us back to reality. This was insane.

He didn't immediately release his hold on me, nor did I want him to. In that moment, the world could have ended, and I wouldn't have given a damn. What was wrong with me? He followed a path of hate and yet...there was no hate between us.

It was at that moment, he removed his mouth from mine and let my legs down, but he didn't let me go. I stood on shaky legs as he rested his head against mine. His body shook. He released his tears. Something was very wrong.

"What...? What happened?"

"My mo...my mother's dead."

"Oh my God! I'm so sorry." I hugged him to me, and he held me tight, his head resting on my shoulder.

"This wasn't supposed—not this—not killing," he whispered.

"Oh, baby, I'm so sorry. Can you tell me what happened?" I didn't want to add to his pain, by telling him that hate and violence leads to only one conclusion.

He raised his head and shifted. I saw the tears shining in his eyes, the fresh tracks on his face.

"I'm sorry. So fucking sorry. I didn't know," he whispered.

I knew what he meant. He was with those assholes.

"They killed my mother, and you could have been fucking hurt too."

"What?"

"My *brothers*, men who I have known for years, guys I

supported, who supported me, killed my mother. *My mom.* It's not like no one knew who she was or where our business was. Something just feels—all wrong."

I was floored. "Wait, how? What?"

"Some of them, created bombs, and those were tossed into the crowds. I had nothing to do with that shit. I swear, I didn't know. One of those Molotov cocktails got thrown into my family's fucking shop. Where my...my mom was standing."

He stepped away from me and leaned against the wall, but he clasped my hand, lacing our fingers together.

"She's dead, they killed her, Harper. Assholes, I have stood with for years, murdered her."

I felt the anger in his words. This time I was the one who turned into him and held him close. My mind raced with what he'd just told me. I might have hated him walking with those Nazis, but he was the one who paid a steep price. "What now? What are you going to do? Will you go to the cops?"

"No cops." He raised his hand and touched the side of my face. "I need to get out of here."

"What about your father? Don't you need to be with him now?"

"I can't... This is my fault. I'm not ready to face him again. He's...he's not a part of this. Besides, *they* are still upstairs waiting on me."

That pissed me off. "Let them wait."

"I need to get out of here."

My phone buzzed. I checked it and saw a text from Serena. Her parents had arrived, and they were ready to leave. I shot her a text letting her know I was on my way back. I'd left my purse with her. I'd go get that and then get Dachs and myself out of there. We needed to talk.. But, not today, tonight, he needed to grieve for his mother.

"Stay right here," I told Dachs. "I'll be right back."

"Where are you going?"

"My friend's here."

His face flushed even more. "Was she hurt from the parade?"

I stared at him. He wasn't the only one suffering from his actions, he needed to know those actions cost a lot of people. "She got a little cut up and has a mild concussion, but they're releasing her right now. Her folks are here to take her home, but she's got my purse. Let me grab it, and then I'll get us out of here."

He took my hand and squeezed it. "I'm sorry. Will she be all right?"

"Yes. She'll be fine."

"Are you sure you want to do this?"

I didn't hesitate. "I'm damn sure."

"Be careful. There are White Pride brothers everywhere here."

I nodded and slipped out the stairwell.

24

DACHS

We escaped through the employee exit through the ER. In all the confusion, no one paid us any attention as we made our way around the building. Harper made arrangements for an Uber that pulled up as we rounded the corner to the entrance. I grabbed the handle and snatched the door open, ushering her in and sliding into the seat beside her.

I glanced at her profile, conflicted. Not that anyone knew about her or where she lived. If anyone saw her with me...a sinking feeling churned in my belly. I'd already been a part of so much destruction. The last thing I wanted to do was bring trouble to Harper's door. The drive was quiet, each of us wrapped up in our thoughts. I pulled my cell free.

I'd left my father alone to deal with my problems. I flipped the device over in my hands and looked over to find Harper peering at me. There was an understanding and genuine kindness in her eyes that I never saw with those men and women I practically grew up with.

She stilled my movements. "Call your dad."

My father was completely alone. My mom's loss sat heavily on my shoulders. Would he blame me for her death?

Harper squeezed my hand in encouragement. "Call him."

I scrolled through the contact list and tapped the screen. The continuous ringing felt never ending. The longer it took for my father to answer, the tighter my chest constricted.

"Hello." My dad's strong, solid tone filled the earpiece.

"Dad," My voice cracked.

"Are you okay? Safe?"

With everything happening, my old man was worried about me? I couldn't hold my misery in any longer. I was an asshole who played a part in my mother's death. "I am s-sorry—s—so very sorry." I leaned forward, curling in on myself, and sobbed.

Harper covered my back with her body, wrapping her arms around my shoulders.

"Son." My dad's tone dropped. "Police are here and although those men have left me alone, I saw one of them loitering near the men's room. Are you safe?"

"Yes."

"You are all I have left. Your mom, she believed in your goodness. You must stay safe."

"I know." I hiccupped. I couldn't stop the flow of tears.

"Everything will be alright. I am okay. This is not your fault. This hatred, Son, it must stop. You cannot go on like this; your mama wouldn't want you to." My father's voice broke. "Cut off your phone and don't let them find you. When I think it's safe, I'll post an open sign on the shop."

"Yes, Sir." My dad had faith in me even though I had no faith in myself. I ended the call.

Harper opened the back door and slid out, tugging me with her.

I didn't realize the car had stopped. I followed without thought. We were in the park at the front of her building. My thoughts were still processing what happened. Why hadn't I caught on to what the Prof and Bruno were up to? A long exhale escaped through my lips. I hung back, our arms extended between us. I should have known. Why was I so damn stupid? I needed to think.

"What's wrong?" Harper turned and closed the gap between us.

I looked around. The sun was shining. Fluffy white clouds rolled across a beautiful light blue sky. Large trees surrounded us; the chirps of birds could be heard. There was no outward sign of the turmoil that had occurred only miles away.

Things weren't sitting right. Where was Bruno? Prof only showed up with a few men, some of them newbies others—they belonged to Gage's chapter. If I didn't do what they asked...*Shit.* I was kept out of the loop for a reason. Was I the end plan, the scapegoat? I shook my head to clear it. "I think I'm being set up."

"What?"

"Too many things are off. I organized the march—everybody knows that." I was quiet for a minute to collect all of my thoughts. "Permits are under the organization name, but Becky, she supports our cause, pulled them. Prof gave Bruno a special project. It was me that did the foot work, though. I made sure we had milk and water in case of pepper-spray, bats and batons to protect ourselves in case we were attacked. I took care of our uniforms, set up the flags and notified each member of their responsibilities. I have organized these events numerous times, big and small. Public disturbance, fights, that I was ready for..."

"Let's go inside. We can talk about this in my condo." She twined her fingers between mine and walked toward the building.

"I don't want you to be hurt. I need to find Bruno."

Or, Becky at the very least.

Somehow, I needed to get to the bottom of this bullshit, now.

Waiting wouldn't work. The Prof had already laid the frame-work, and hell if I would bend over and let the SOB continue to fuck me. "I need to leave. I have to find them."

She shook her head. "What are you talking about? Find who?"

"I have to go." I pulled my hand free. I couldn't—wouldn't give Harper problems. First, I had to sort out the mess I suspected was waiting for me. Who knew what the Prof would do if I couldn't be found.

"Whatever is going on in your head, stop it. Let's go home and talk. I need to understand what is happening and what you're thinking."

"I can't hurt anyone else." I hung my head.

The pain and remorse of what I'd done morphed into anger. The overwhelming feeling that my brothers had betrayed me riled in my belly. I'd be damned if I would let them ruin anymore of my life.

"It will be alright. We will figure this out."

I wasn't ready to walk away, but I understood what needed to happen. It could very well come down to me walking into a police station and telling them everything. I shook my head. Snitching—that wasn't something I would do. This—this situa-tion I would handle it my way. Putting Harper in the middle of that wasn't right. I was a bastard but not that much of a bastard —yet. I reclaimed her hand. "We have tonight." Tomorrow I would start the hunt for the assholes I was sure were trying to fuck me.

Gage.

I might not be able to find the key players of this bullshit fiasco, but Gage, he wasn't the type to hide.

I stared down at Harper. From our first meeting, she'd gotten under my skin. The last thing I wanted to do was lose her before we even really began. The only way to keep her and my dad safe, might be by walking away.

She held my gaze for a long time.

"Let's go to your place." I couldn't smile. So many dark thoughts in my head made it hard—impossible to feel anything but negativity. I didn't know how to reassure her.

She cocked her head to the side, and her dreads brushed her shoulders. I reached out and fingered it. Its softness tickled my fingers, continuing to surprise me. Yeah, I would give myself one more night with Harper, then I would have to make some hard decisions.

"I really need you right now." And, I did. I didn't want to think about all the bullshit that happened to me in the last twelve hours. I didn't want to feel all the emotions that threatened to overtake me. I had to be smart and take control of the situation I'd been put in. The only person who would get this now was Harper.

After tonight though, I would find Gage, Becky or Bruno. Somebody was going to explain to me what the fuck happened. Those bastards owed me for the death of my mother and all of them would pay. I didn't have to go searching for the Prof just yet. That fucker would be easy to find, and he would be the last man I went after. I exhaled and followed Harper into the building.

25

HARPER

I opened my condo and entered first, holding the door open so Dachs could come in behind me. I turned to shut the door as soon as he entered but found myself crowded against it, face first. The coolness of the wood bled into my cheek.

What was it about this man? One look, one touch from him and my common sense—hell, anything having to do with intellect, flew right out the window—far and fast. I doubted it would return anytime soon. Damnit, we needed to talk. If he thought I'd let him handle this by himself, he had another thing coming. Then, he ground himself against my ass.

Okay. Talk later.

Right now, all I could concentrate on was the feel of him pressed against me.

He took my hands, and my purse dropped to the floor. He raised my hands above my head and held them against the wood as he pressed his body into mine.

Sweet Jesus!

My eyes drifted shut as I fell head first into the pleasure coursing throughout my body as he pushed against me. None of last night had been my imagination. The current driving us to each other was as strong as ever—maybe even stronger.

I could feel the length of his all too familiar cock pressing into my ass. So, I pushed back. He moved one of his hands but continued to hold onto both of mine. That free hand of his moved my jacket aside and roamed down the side of my sweater until he got his hand under it and touched my skin.

Well damn.

His ungloved hand was cool against my body, but that's not what caused my shudder. That would be the spark inside me he started. Slowly, he glided that hand higher until his thumb brushed against the side of my bra, seeking until he could rub it over my nipples. I moaned.

"You like that?"

"You know I do. More," I managed to get out.

I felt his leg between my thighs, nudging mine farther apart, then he moved his hand down the front of my body, looking for a button on my pants, I guessed but these were leggings. I like leggings and stretchy jeans. He must have figured that out because he slid his hand inside the stretchy waistband and moved it downward.

His fingers spanned out, and he stroked me. "Have mercy. You're wet already, baby."

I grinned. I was bare. I already knew from last night how much he liked it. Most men did.

Then I felt his thumb. He flicked it against my clit, then pressed against it. My pussy spasmed.

"My God. I need you," Dachs groaned against my ear.

He slid a finger inside me, and I sunk down into him, trying to get more of his finger. He pushed up and pulled down to meet my movements. He released my hands, so he could move the hair away from my neck; he buried his face against it and rubbed against me. He continued to stroke his finger in and out of me.

"Love the way you fucking smell. You took a bath this morning. I can't smell me on you anymore. I want your scent all over me. I will put mine all over you."

"Yes, Dammit, yes."

I turned my head toward him. It was awkward, but our lips managed to connect. Our tongues played around each other, but it wasn't enough. We both needed so much more. I know I did. In seconds his finger was out of me. I felt its absence more than I could have ever imagined. He quickly spun me around to face him and bending, effortlessly, picked me up.

"Bedroom," I whispered.

The low lights under the kitchen cabinets were on, providing enough light to see the kitchen area but also enough to show him the way. There were several doors in the room; he knew which one was my bedroom. It was a two-bedroom condo, so he didn't have far to walk. I wrapped my arms around him as he strode to my bedroom door. It wasn't closed all the way, and he used his foot to shove it open more.

He moved right for the bed and placed me on it. He hovered briefly over me. Shadows ventured in this room—too many. I needed to see him and told him so. Last night we came together in a dark room. Now, I wanted us to see each other, open fully, nothing hidden—no secrets, just the two of us.

"I want to see you, open the drapes."

Dachs glanced over at the windows that were on either side of the bed and did as I asked. I kicked off my shoes and settled against the pillows on my king sized bed. I like a lot of room and the bedroom was large enough that it fit.

Light spilled in. I didn't worry about neighbors. I was on the twentieth floor, and the nearest building as tall as this one was a block over. But, the light that filtered in now was more than enough for me to see the desire in Dachs' eyes. I smiled when he sat on the bed and reached out to grab one of my locks. He rubbed it between his fingers then tightened his hold on it, tugging slightly to draw me toward him.

"You are so damn beautiful."

He placed his lips over mine, claiming me once more. I felt his hand at the back of my head sealing me to him. He tasted like everything I'd ever wanted in my life. After everything that went on today, how was this happening? I didn't know nor did I care. I couldn't. This was about us, no one else. He needed me tonight. There was no hate in this room.

He pulled back, and I followed him, but his hands moved to my shirt, and he took it off. I reached around to undo my bra and dropped it on the cover. His eyes immediately zeroed in on my nipples. My chest rose and fell in reaction to that look.

"So beautiful." He raised his hand and touched my left breast with his thumb. Circling the areole, before holding it in his hand. Leaning forward, he encircled it with his mouth and began to lick it with the tip of his tongue.

I moaned again, and this time, I was the one holding his head to me. I tilted my head back and settled more comfortably into my bed. I felt him sitting up, and I opened my eyes to pull him back, but he only moved to unlace his boots. I sat up and tugged his jacket off, then reached for his shirt. Slow is all well and good, and I like slow. Right now, though, I wanted him out of that white shirt. The shirt that still smelled a little like smoke and had a spot of blood. At least he wasn't wearing those heinous red suspenders. I didn't want to think about the smoke, the blood or any of it. Those things had no place here—not with us, not now, not ever again.

I began tugging at that shirt, but he had to unbutton it. I think he might have been in a rush too because I think he might have popped a couple of the buttons. His mouth clamped onto mine again as we reached for each other, unable to be apart for even a second more than we had to be.

His hands moved to my leggings to pull them off me, and my hands moved to his waist to find his belt and tug it off. I raised my legs to help him get my leggings off one leg, and he shifted so I could unzip him. But we both had to stop touching each other for a moment, so he could get his damn pants off, and I could lose the leggings.

He pulled my underwear off until we were both naked. My eyes roamed over the ink on his skin; I hadn't really been able to see much last night. Most of it was beautiful, the Celtic crosses over both halves of his chest and the bands on his biceps. He sat near my waist and just stared at me. My attention was diverted when his cock twitched. He was long, thick, and hard. I started to reach toward him, to touch him, but then he stretched out beside me. We both turned to face each other. He placed his hand on my hip. When he stared at me with a storm in his azure eyes, I knew that this time, what we were about to do, what we were about to become, would change both of our lives. I reached for him and drew him to me because this was what I always knew we would be.

When he slid into my canal we both breathed a sigh of relief. His body in mine felt like I was welcoming him home. I opened for him, knowing I always would.

He nudged his arms under my legs, spreading me wider for him while he nestled over me. His lips captured mine, and my eyes fluttered as he flexed forward, filling me completely. I could feel his cock throbbing against my inner walls, and I shuddered against him. He paused for a moment, and then, he began to move—long slow strokes at first, pulling out not quite to his tip before pushing forward again. I moaned, tightening my ass and shifting my hips upward, trying to get him to move forward faster. The feel of his mouth over mine lessened slightly as I could feel him smile against my lips. I opened my eyes, and he pulled back staring at me.

Dachs held my gaze as he surged all the way in until he could go no farther. Yet, he'd gone farther than anyone ever had because he touched my heart. It thumped against my chest, for a moment I couldn't breathe. My eyes filled with tears, but they were ones of joy, I smiled up at him. I let him see me, who I really was, and as I looked at him, I saw his heart in his eyes too.

He kissed the tears from my eyes, rubbed his cheek against mine and then he began to move. His strokes came faster and stronger than they had before, and I moved with him. A storm broke inside us, our cries rose in synchronicity, in a day of such sadness, these were ones filled with hope and satisfaction. Together we created our own tempest that no one and nothing could stop. A promise was made then, silent but real.

Nothing could stand between us. He is mine.

26

DACHS

Sunlight poured through the windows and illuminated Harper's body. Under the beams, her tanned skin was radiant. I gazed down my body; her arm lay wrapped around my middle, and her face was buried against my neck. A thin sheet draped across our waists. I eased from her embrace, sliding to the edge of the mattress. It—no—she was becoming a habit, and I didn't want to leave but knew I had to.

It wasn't right starting something with Harper when I was mired in this bullshit. First, I needed to check on my dad. I knew what he meant about staying away, but he was all I had left. No way was I going to abandon him. Then I needed to track down Becky. She would probably be easier to find than fuckboy Bruno or Gage. I am no snitch, but I had one Hail Mary option. If all else failed, then I would walk through the damn doors of a police station and turn state's evidence. Whatever it took to keep the ones I love safe even if it meant disappearing and becoming a puppet for the fucked up judicial system.

I lifted Harper's arm up by the wrist and laid it on the spot I had occupied. A sense of déjà vu shuttered through me. It took some time to find my clothes, still it didn't take as much time as the day before. The urge to wake her was overwhelming. I needed to get out of there, fast, or I wouldn't leave. I dressed in the living room and searched for paper and a pen. I found a loose sheet lodged between a stack of books and a pencil beside them.

There are some things I need to take care of. I'll call you later. How did I end the note? *Tell her I love her*? Did I even know what that was? Things were moving fast...I wanted to protect her, keep her with me. Was that love? I shook my head. I was making things more complicated than they were. There was no time to think about it. She was important to me, and that was what counted. I signed the note with a simple *D*. I slipped from her condo and once again felt like a thief for sneaking away.

In the elevator I pulled my phone free and tapped the screen, searching for my dad's number in my contact list. I know he didn't want me to contact him, but how could I not? It rang through to voicemail. I moved on and found Becky's number. She picked up on the second ring.

"Hello." Her voice was shaky. "Dachs?"

"Where the fuck is Bruno?" The elevator doors slid open, and I stepped into the lobby and marched through the exit.

"I don't know." She paused. "Prof is looking for you."

"You knew, didn't you?" She had to. If we were in the same fucking room together I would strangle the bitch.

"I didn't know someone would die."

"That *someone* was my mom. My *mom*." Pain morphed to fury and sizzled through my being. I resisted the urge to run. I couldn't move fast enough. "How could you not? They were fucking bombs!" My voice rose. I had to look around to make sure I wasn't drawing attention to myself. I trotted down the street. The subway was a couple of blocks away. "Where are you?"

"The police picked me up yesterday. I spent the night being

interrogated. I just got home. Prof will be proud. I didn't tell them anything." Becky was rambling. "They tried to say we're terrorists. I told them they were wrong. We are exercising our right to protect our race."

A thought struck me. Did I sound this damn crazy? I had to keep her calm or else I wouldn't get the information I needed. "Where is the Prof?" I was going to find someone, today. "Gage?"

"I don't know, haven't seen the Prof since yesterday afternoon." she sobbed. "All I did was sign my name to a piece of paper. I didn't do anything. I didn't hurt anybody!"

Becky was losing her shit. I sucked in a breath, tapping my anger down. "I know you didn't, babe. I really need to talk to someone, Bruno, maybe. Do you have any idea where he might have gone?" Bruno was wanted for a murder charge in Jersey, so he wouldn't go home—or would he? The best way to hide was in plain sight.

"I only did what I was told," she repeatedly mumbled.

Becky was a victim as much as I was and her indoctrination to the Prof went a shitload deeper than mine did. Talking to Becky wouldn't get me anywhere. I ended the call. It was better to face the devil head on. Change of plans. I scrolled down the contact list and tapped the Prof's number. He answered right away.

"It's about time you called me. Where are you?"

My mentor was too calm. A niggle of distrust fluttered at the back of my mind. "I'm around." I knew the fucker well. He must have had several plans figured out and only God knew which one he was on.

Tread carefully.

The words scrolled through my head.

"The police are looking for you."

"Funny, I heard it was you searching for me. Where's Bruno?" I didn't have time to play games.

"I know you didn't mean for any of this to happen but, son, you need to contact the police and sort everything out. Explain how you planned the attack with a few other group members. The police already know everything."

WTF? "We both know who did what." I needed to cut the call short. A faint click piggy backed our conversation. Was the line tapped? The bastard needed to die. "I'm coming for you." I pulled the cell from my ear, and my finger hovered over the screen.

"Wait!"

I could feel the set-up. Knew in my heart Prof was saving his own skin.

"You want me. Come get me. I am at the headquarters."

I stabbed the end button. Cell phones could easily be traced. Prof had already set up his alibi and most likely laid everything down at mine and Bruno's feet. I yanked the sim card free from my cell and dropped it in the trash. If my phone happened to fall into anyone else's hands they wouldn't have access to my contact list. Then I turned off my phone before I entered the subway station. I was foolish for making the calls, and I would pay for it. My stupidity in general was fucking epic. I snagged a seat at the end of the car with my back to the wall and could easily see who was coming and going.

I dropped my head back and listened to the scrub of metal against metal, letting the gentle rocking soothe my troubled mind. Something wasn't right. Prof—there was something wrong with him. He spoke calmly, but I'd swear he was anxious. It was something I couldn't quite put my finger on.

Thoughts tumbled about in my head. I wanted to kill my mentor for what he'd done. Fuck that, everyone involved in my mother's death needed to die. Her gentle face floated before my eyes then vanished just as quickly. Killing them wouldn't bring her back. I couldn't kill all of them, but I needed to clear my name. *Bruno.* It was open season on that fat fuck when I found him. Becky, she—she was screwed in the head,, and there was no telling when, if ever, she would come back to herself. Gage, who knew where that asshole stood or just how deeply he was involved. That only left me and Prof to set shit straight, and I'd be damned if I was taking the fall for the bastard.

The garbled announcement of my stop tumbled from the overhead speakers. I stood as the train came to a stop. People crowded the exit. Someone was watching a news segment on their phone. I caught the tail end of the words.

Police are searching for key members of a white supremacy organization thought to be behind yesterday's fire bombings during the Martin Luther King Parade. Names are currently being withheld, and a news conference is planned for this afternoon. Authorities have cited a person of interest in custody they have yet to name. The attack killed a local businesswoman...

The doors swished open, and I was ushered out with the crowd. Who the hell did the cops have in custody? I spoke to Prof and Becky. The only two people I wasn't able to contact were Bruno and Gage. I was sure they had both already skipped town. Could one of them have been caught so quickly? I trudged my way up the familiar street. Nothing seemed out of place and still everything felt wrong. I couldn't shake the unwavering feeling I was being watched. I stopped in front of the building that housed our headquarters. The place where Bruno slept. Was I walking into a trap? I rolled my shoulders and exhaled. Of course, I was; I wasn't so foolish as to not see the path the Prof was leading me down. This set up—I would play it out to the fucking end. I trotted up the steps and into the building.

I didn't knock. I twisted the knob, and the door opened effortlessly into the first floor apartment. Prof sat in a wingback chair by the window. The same seat I held during the jump in celebration a few days ago. God, but it felt more like years.

"You got here faster than I thought you would." Prof twisted to face me but didn't rise from his seat.

I didn't care to make small talk. "Where is Bruno?" He made the Molotov cocktails. I had no doubt in my mind he was the one who tossed them. Even with the Prof in front of me, Bruno was the son of a bitch I wanted to get a hold of first. If the Prof couldn't give me an answer, it didn't look like I would have a choice. I snorted, plans to fit my situation were changing in my head. After I beat the shit out of Bruno I would drag his ass to the police. Killing him wouldn't work when I needed the bastard to clear my name. But the Prof? Maybe I wouldn't need Bruno. The Prof could explain his fucked up ideas to the police, which gave me the freedom to simply kill the Jersey boy. So many ways for things to go. The shitty organization was rotten, and my mother deserves justice. Even me, I wasn't negligent in this bull-shit. Every one of us needed to pay a price. I'd already lost so much, I just wasn't sure exactly how much more I needed to pay.

"You would know better than me since you two planned this."

I snapped my head up. This lying son of a bitch. I took a step forward, my hands closing into fists.

Be calm, Dachs. Answers first.

I could hear Harper's voice in my head. "Becky pulled the permits. I organized the event. Made sure we had our uniforms, water and milk. Flags for the march. But you—you gave Bruno a special project. I should have pushed harder to find out what that was." I pressed my lips together to keep from lashing out.

"Stop trying to place the blame on everybody but yourself. You murdered your mother." Prof scooted to the edge of the chair. "It's okay, Dachs. I'll get the best lawyers for you and the brothers who helped you. Your dedication to the cause is admirable."

"You will not pin this on me." I ground out between

clenched teeth. "Your actions killed my mother!" I inched closer, balling up my fists tighter as I moved. "Me...Becky...we had nothing to do with your grandiose plans to make America white again." A bark of laughter escaped me as I realized the irony of it all. Actually, we did, I just never anticipated murder. "You wanted to destroy a few blacks, and instead, killed a lone white woman—my fucking mother, you rank bastard!" It was harder to control my emotions than I thought.

"Just admit your mistake, and we can work everything else out." Prof leaned forward. Silence settled in around us.

It would only take a couple of steps to close the gap between us. I stopped. "I am not the one who did this. I neither planned nor executed your fucked up plot. I would have stopped it." My words ended in a whisper. Then louder, "You know that. I believed in separating the races, not killing them." I shook my head and realization dawned on me like a lightning strike. The person of interest was Prof. But if he was the one...shouldn't he be in jail? He was trying to offset the blame on me and the others. This putrid asshole was going to accept his responsibility.

I lunged for him, catching him by the shirt and hefting him up on his toes. He didn't fight back. "You motherfucker. You're wired." I plowed a fist into his jaw. He stumbled back into the wall. My grip loosened, and I tried to keep my balance, shifting forward to close the space that sprung between us. I yanked him up and punched him in the belly. Red splotches blossomed on his face. He clutched my wrists, holding on to them as our movements formed a macabre dance. The feeling of wrongness amplified. I shuffled back, jerking my arms to break free.

Doors busted open. Cops in riot gear flowed through the open doorways converging on us. Prof looked up at me, and a sly smile lifted the corners of his mouth. In that moment, everything made sense. The way he separated the groups, keeping everyone in the dark. His refusal to fight, the asshole had already spun lies and fed them to the authorities. It was my intention to keep this bullshit within our group. Maintain the honor the fucking liar had preached to us until we took his damn words as gospel.

Cops yanked me back; he was pulled from my clutches. The shrewd look in his eyes, how had I missed that? I was thrown to the floor, my arms wrenched behind me. My face shoved into the filthy rug, grime rubbing against my cheek. Particles of waste tickling my nostrils. The click of cuffs, another layer of noise that burst through the room. He'd organized everything right down to an escape plan and everyone would think it was me, but I wasn't the snitch. The man that I'd looked up to like a father at one time—*he was.*

27

DACHS

I wasn't a stranger to the booking process. Electronic fingerprinting, mugshot, other than an upgrade in technology everything remained the same, except for the DNA swab. That's new, but then again it had been a while since I'd been arrested. Walking down the long corridor gave me time to think, until arraignment I'd be in a holding cell. At least until the damn detectives decided to have a chat with me. After booking, I should be able to make my phone call—to Harper. By the time everything played out, if she found me a lawyer, he should be at the station.

Metal scrapped as the clear door rolled to the side. I stepped over the threshold into the empty cell, benches built into the walls, everything washed in a pale green color. A steel toilet and sink tucked in the corner and open for all to see completed the space. I dropped down on a spot closest to the door and stretched my legs out. I held on to the hope that the Prof would accidentally be booked into the same holding cell. The squeak of the rollers moving the door drew my attention back to the room's entrance. I rose, anticipation sharpening my senses. A plain clothes cop stepped through the doorway and met my stare. I held his gaze.

"I'm Detective Mitchell, want to talk?" Older, deep wrinkles etched his withered face. An almost white mustache covered his top lip and bushy salt and pepper brows were above his clear, knowledgeable blue eyes.

This cop was no fool. My hopes at meeting Prof again were dashed. "Sure, lets chat." I shifted to the side and caught a glimpse of who had to be the old man's black partner. The coldness of the black guy's gaze wasn't lost on me. Hate recognized hate. I felt his rage down to my soul, and I understood it. I knew exactly what he was feeling toward me, shit I was experiencing all these damn emotions about myself. The detective spun on his heel and left, and I followed. In the hallway two uniformed policemen were waiting to handcuff me.

Through the maze of passageways, down a flight of stairs, I was led to an interrogation room at the end of the dank hall. I peered through the doorway. A table was stuffed into the corner of the tiny room with two chairs on the free side of the furniture piece. There was just enough room for him and the other two men to fit —which meant they would probably tag me, good cop, bad cop. I snorted. It would be interesting to see who played which role.

The black man strolled into the room first and claimed a chair, settling into it. "Have a seat."

So this was how it was going to play out. I glanced up at Mitchell; he was already moving away down the hall. The guards removed my cuffs and backed up, and I stepped into the Lion's Den. The door closed with a quiet click. I checked the ceiling and corners. No tell-tell black globes. The interview was being recorded though; I would bet on it.

I sat, quietly waiting. My rage wasn't directed at the cops. I had to be smart about how and what I did and said. I wouldn't continue to be a pawn in some unknown game. We peered at each for long moments. I guess that was supposed to make me uncomfortable.

"You got something you want to get off your chest. Don't you?"

His cajoling tone was annoying. "No, I did nothing wrong."

"The victim. She was your mother, right? Not only did you commit an act of terrorism, but you killed the woman that birthed you."

I crossed my arms and uncrossed them. I couldn't let anger get the best of me. My wrong was following blindly behind a man I trusted. I waited until my rage subsided before I spoke. "My mother was murdered, but I had no hand in it."

"We have witness testimony that you marched right along with your little group. The members we spoke with say you organized the march. Is everyone lying?" The cop cocked his head to the side.

Yeah, they probably were to protect the Prof. I sighed. Me and this guy weren't going to get very far. "I had nothing to do with the bombing."

"Want to know how many times I have heard that in my career?"

"Not really." This was just another reason why I didn't trust the legal system. Cops had formed an opinion before they ever knew the facts. All just because they didn't like the person they thought was the criminal. Meanwhile, the fuckers that actually committed the crime are walking scot free.

"You think you're a hardass?"

This bullshit was almost comical. I shifted in my seat, scooting down. "No." If they couldn't solve my problem, I would. I just needed the right time. "Where is the Prof?"

"Who?" The cop leaned forward and rested his arms on the

table. "Oh, you mean one of your co-conspirators? He's down the hall with my partner telling us all about you."

"He's a lying asshole, and you're the dumbasses for buying into his shit." I let my emotions get the best of me for a minute. "Make you no better than me for buying into his bullshit." How long would this bs go on. If they sent us both to jail at least I would have a chance to get the bastard. Snitching on the people —my brothers—wouldn't do anyone any good. Not when the real mastermind was walking around. First, I was set up and now it's like the fucker is getting farther away from me.

"Tell me your story." The policeman's voice softened. He pressed his lips together forming a frown,, and kindness replaced anger so clear in his eyes only moments ago.

I wanted to burst out in laughter at the situation. It wasn't two cops playing at good cop bad cop it's one detective with a bi-polar disorder. "I trusted the wrong people. End of story." We could go on like this forever. Was it beneficial for me to stay here in interrogation or shut it down by asking for a lawyer? Either way I was no longer sure I could get to the motherfuckers that killed my mom. I couldn't afford to play with these assholes anymore. Prof wouldn't stop at killing my mom. He would try to make an example of my dad as a warning to me. At least that is what I would do. No one was protecting my father. I couldn't get to my old mentor right away now anyway. I would have to think of another way.

"I want a lawyer." I quietly uttered the words. It was up to the authorities now. Indict me or let me go in twenty-four hours. Hopefully, Harper would take care of my request.

28

HARPER

What was it about this man leaving me in the morning—twice in two days? I was going to put a stop to that. I read Dachs' note again as I stood in front of my window, staring out onto the scene of the city below. Everything moved as it did most days. But today was different—I was different. I'd tried to reach him, of course, as soon as I'd gotten up a few hours ago. His side of the bed had still been warm with his heat. I'd even put off taking a shower because I wanted to carry his scent on me for as long as I could. But, I had to get up and take a shower. Too bad it was alone. I wondered when he'd call me? I hoped his dad was doing okay. I felt sure he was with him. I lost my mom when I was young, but I still remembered her and still missed her. I couldn't imagine losing a mother the way Dachs had to such violence.

My thoughts were broken when my cell phone rang. I picked it up from the coffee table hoping it was Dachs. Instead, it was an unfamiliar number, but caller ID indicated it was from the city jail. Frowning, I answered it.

"Collect call from Dachs Neuman. Say or press 1 for yes, or say or press 2 for no."

"Yes. Oh God. Yes."

"Listen."

"Dachs, what in the name of Jesus is going on?"

"*Listen*. I've been arrested."

I glanced at the phone for a second. "You've got to be fucking kidding me."

"Harper," he uttered my name quietly. "I can't call my dad, but I'm going to need a lawyer. I have money, so I can pay. I don't want any damn public defender. Everything was...set up. I figured you'd know a good lawyer."

"You're damn right I do."

"Okay, good."

He told me where they were holding him, and I took down the information.

"Just send him down here, and I'll take care of everything else here."

"Okay, I'll see you—"

"No. Stay out of this. I gotta go. Just send him, sweetheart. I'll call you again as soon as I can."

When Dachs hung up, I immediately called the lawyer in my contact list my father has on retainer and gave him the information Dachs gave me. He was the named partner in one of the best law firms in Boston, and they handled everything. If he couldn't do this, he'd send one of his associates who did. I told him where to meet me. We were making another stop first. If Dachs thought I'd stay out of this Mr. Man had another think coming. But, he'd learn; I sat in the back for no one.

Next, I made another call. This one to my father's golf buddy, who happened to be the Chief of Police; my dad was one of his biggest supporters. Then, I got dressed. Dachs might not want me there, but we meant something to each other, and after last night, I was going to be damned if I let him go through this alone—not when I knew I could help. I called an Uber.

When Dachs' lawyer arrived, I'd just sat down with the Chief. I smiled when I saw who walked into the office. I'd met Donald at a few functions my father had hosted. He was also one of the partners in the firm and he was black. Of course, he and the Chief already knew each other. I chuckled to myself at the irony of him defending a white nationalist.

"Let me tell you a story, full disclosure, the story is about my boyfriend. I tell you that so you will understand the depth of what's going on here. He is a white nationalist or was." Was he my boyfriend? Well, he was now, and he better leave that other crap behind.

I explained to them both what I knew about Dachs. To say their eyes opened wide at those revelations would have been hysterical if it wasn't so serious. I also told them what I suspected, he was being set up and who might really be behind the bomb that killed his mother. I gave them the names of two people on campus who could verify what I told them. "Professor Sharpe was not only in the forefront of that march but is a leader in that organization. He likes to brag and or recruit. He wasn't as careful around campus as he thought he was. His leanings were well known on campus. He's actively tried to recruit one of my white classmates and had actually recruited one of my classmate's younger brothers. If anyone was behind the bombing and the death of Dachs' mother, it was that fuckwit."

Both men listened, then the Chief asked us to give him a minute while he made some phone calls. Donald and I stepped out of the room while he made the calls. I was so nervous. A jail, even if it was just the administrative office section of their headquarters, was not a place I'd ever thought I'd see the inside of. I took the opportunity to use the ladies room and when I got back the Chief was ready for us. By the frown on his face, I knew none of it would be good.

"First off, I've just spoken to both the detective who arrested Mr. Neuman as well as the FBI agent in charge."

"The FBI? Why?" I asked shocked.

Donald answered, "domestic terrorism."

"What?"

Chief nodded his head. "Yes, they're still investigating the circumstances around the bombing and are holding your friend, Mr. Neuman, for questioning. I also passed along the information you gave me."

The beat of my heart drummed against my ears. This can't be happening. "I don't understand. Why is the FBI involved? How is this domestic terrorism?" I glanced at Donald.

"It may be because an explosion was involved. Section 802 of the USA Patriot Act, essentially covers domestic terrorism. A section of Title 18 of the US Code is used when a bomb is involved. And section F would also be triggered, since the explosion took place in a public place," Donald offered.

"But Dachs had nothing to do with any bomb. Marching yes, bombs no. It was his parents' store for Christ sake where they tossed the bomb that killed his mother," I argued.

"Still, I find it interesting the FBI is involved. From my understanding, it was just a Molotov cocktail used, something anyone can make from easily accessible ingredients, so not sure why it's not a state criminal matter being used to prosecute," Donald stated.

The Chief leaned forward in his chair. "All of which is still under investigation. I will tell you this. The FBI had that particular branch of troublemakers under watch for quite some time. Which is why they're involved."

"I don't care who's involved," I said. "Will Dachs be charged with anything?"

"It's still too early to say. But he will be held for at least 24-

hours while we try to determine his role, if any, surrounding the circumstances of the explosion and subsequent loss of life."

The more he spoke the more pissed off I became. The circumstances were Dachs mother was killed, and his so called friends were behind it, but *he's* the one sitting in jail.

"Well my understanding is Mr. Neuman has already been questioned and has asked for representation. I am letting you know I now represent him and once we leave here, will file the necessary paperwork. I expect to be able to speak to the agent in charge or detective as well as my client today and we'll take it from there." Donald's words were strongly worded statements.

"Is there anything you can do to help expedite things?" I asked the Chief. "To get him the hell out of jail right friggin now."

"I'll go down to the station with you and see if I can smooth things over."

I accompanied Donald and the Chief to the district where Dachs was being held. I stayed in a waiting area while the Chief and Donald had a chat with the detective and the agent in charge before Donald got to speak with Dachs. I'd been waiting for over an hour when my phone rang. It was Selena. I answered and told her everything, right down to me sleeping with Dachs twice, and I planned on doing it again and again and then some. She was my best friend; she needed to know and either she stood by me, or she showed me who she really was.

She didn't disappoint.

"I'll be right down. I'll wait with you."

"That's it."

"Nothing more to be said. You need me, I'm there."

This is why I loved her, and she was my best friend. "No. Really, I'll be fine. We both will."

"So, do you love him?"

"Yes." I didn't even have to think about it. I didn't add 'I think I always have.' Too unreal. "But I haven't told him yet."

"Then, I've got to meet this guy soon. He better be good to you and out of that shit for real or else I'll kick his ass."

"And I'll help you."

"Well, from his actions, he might just love you."

I smiled because I thought the same thing. "How are you feeling?"

"I'm fine." We stayed on the phone for a while longer.

"Call me after you leave there," Serena said.

"I will, thank you."

I waited a few hours. The Chief dropped in to check on me twice, but he wouldn't tell me anything other than 'they were working things out' and that 'Donald was one hell of a lawyer.' Given the gravity of the involvement of the FBI, I was worried about Dachs, but knew he was in good hands with Donald.

Four hours after I'd gotten there, the Chief and Donald came back.

"That's an interesting young man you got there," Donald said.

"Where is he? Can I see him? Has he been arrested?"

"No, you won't be able to see him. They need to check out a few things, but I'm confident he won't be charged in connection with the bombing. Doesn't mean he's entirely clear, but he should be released in the morning," Donald said.

DACHS WASN'T RELEASED until later the next day, but I was waiting for him when he was—just thankful he had been. I found Donald and Dachs standing in front of the reception counter. Dachs looked up and saw me. He smiled, then, I was in his arms.

I didn't care who saw us together; he held me to him and pressed his lips against mine. Us together was everything. Dachs didn't seem to care much either.

Hand in hand, Donald got us out of there. His car was waiting in the front, and we all got in.

Unable to keep silent any longer, I turned from Dachs and asked, "What happened? Has he been charged?"

Donald answered, "No, for now, he hasn't been charged with anything. However, the Professor, or should I say Mr. Dwight, has been under investigation by the FBI for a few years now. Six years ago, there was a similar type of bomb used in a march Mr. Dwight was involved in, upstate. They just couldn't get anything to stick to him. But thanks to what the ongoing investigation has managed to uncover, along with Dachs' statements, they may be charging him with the murder of Dachs' mother."

"Wait, why did you say 'Mr. Dwight?'" I asked.

"Well, turns out he's not an actual professor. Stephen B. Sharpe is an alias. Kevin Dwight is his real name. The two works he's published had been plagiarized. Harvard discovered that several months ago and quietly fired him."

"What?"

"He's a coward, a liar and an asshole, so doesn't surprise me at all," Dachs said.

I shook my head, but like Dachs, nothing about that man surprised me anymore.

"He tried to tell the cops I planned the attack. Fucker even wore a wire to try to get me to confess."

"What you said during that discussion is what helped to convince the investigators that Dwight was behind it all," Donald added. "He should be arraigned sometime today."

"Good! About Bruno?" Dachs asked, squeezing my hand. "That bastard—he made and threw the cocktails."

"There's an APB out on him. He'll be charged too," Donald

said. "There were several witnesses and apparently a video that showed Mr. Matte tossing lighted bottles into the crowd."

"Yeah. Good luck finding him. My guess is he went back home, to Jersey. He's the type to run. He knows he can't stay here any longer," Dachs said. "If I catch him..."

I stared at him hard. "You'll call the cops and have them arrest him." I did not want Dachs doing anything that would land him back in jail.

"I have to warn you. Even if they catch Bruno, the one the cops really want is Dwight; if Bruno cooperates he might be able to make a plea for a lighter sentence, you may not be entirely off the hook."

"How is that even possible?" I asked. "Dachs only participated in the march. While all of it might have been this Dwight's idea, it was Bruno who threw the bomb purposely into Dachs' parents store that killed his mom. Bruno had to have known exactly what he was doing and whose business was going to be hurt by it," I argued.

"I'm not saying Dachs will be charged with anything, the agent seemed hesitant about pursuing charges against Dachs nor am I certain Bruno will get a deal. Only that it's a possibility."

"He'll never turn on the Prof," Dachs said, shaking his head. "That fucker is his idol."

"Maybe, but the prosecutor can be very persuasive. Massachusetts might not have the death penalty, but Bruno will be charged under Federal jurisdiction and Capital Punishment can be placed on the table. Even without Bruno turning on Mr. Dwight I think the prosecutor can build a solid case against both men for the murder of your mother," Donald said.

Neither of us said another word but from the tenseness in Dachs frame, I knew he didn't like the sound of even the possibility of Bruno getting away with anything. I laid my head on his shoulder, hoping we'd get through this.

Donald dropped us off at my condo and told Dachs he'd call him tomorrow to iron out some details about his deal with the cops and to keep him abreast of any developments.

We rode up the elevator in silence, but his arm remained wrapped around my shoulders and mine around his waist. We entered my condo, and he trudged toward the couch. "You okay?" I asked.

He ran his hand through his hair. "I need to call my father."

"Of course. He must be worried sick."

"Yeah. Can I borrow your phone? Police still have mine."

29

DACHS

I stared out the picture window of Harper's place into the night. Concentric circles of lights brushed away the darkness, creating new art on a blank, black canvas. The past few eye-opening days felt like a lifetime. Harper slipped her arms around me from behind and rested her head on my back, between my shoulder blades. I repressed a snort. This woman was my catalyst for change. Her skin color no longer mattered to me. When shit hit the wall she was the one to stand with me. A black woman. Not my supposed Aryan brothers or even the undercover fringe supporters. In that moment when I was waiting in the lobby—I was waiting for Harper; that realization struck me like a bolt of lightning. In that moment I understood, my mom was right, and I had wasted so many years not listening to her. The hate needed to stop.

It was time to start fresh. Tomorrow was a new day. I covered Harper's hands with my own and held them. I still had classes and work. It was surreal that my life for the most part would return to normal tomorrow.

"What's on your mind?" I could feel her breath flow across my skin through my shirt.

So many thoughts screamed for attention in my head. *Guilt* washed through me. I needed to call my dad, and stroking Harper's hand, I realized she held her cell. I slipped it from her fingers. I wasn't embarrassed to talk with my father, but in standing next to Harper those arguments, the hate I spewed, I felt shame for the first time in my life. The wrongness of it all weighed heavy on my shoulders—in my soul.

"I'm going to call my dad." I pulled free of her embrace, inching away from her. I looked at the screen and held up her cell. "Can you unlock it for me?" She stabbed the screen with her finger, a certain look defining her features—sort of like my mom used to give me. The turn down corners of her mouth and hooded look as she watched me, as if silently questioning if I was an idiot. "Thanks." I dialed my dad's number from memory.

"Hello." There was a bit of hesitation to the old man's tone.

"Dad." I wanted to say so much and knew I couldn't. Not yet. It was more important to hear his voice.

"I was—am worried about you. I saw the news."

"I'm okay. Everything is fine." I could explain better in person. "Mom—umm—what are you doing? What—how? We don't have any family…"

"What are you talking about, Son? We have each other."

Why didn't I listen? I'd missed out on so many years. "I have money to help bury her—to lay mom to rest." I'd been saving money since I started working at fifteen. At first it was errands for Prof; he would entice me with pocket money. A hundred here, another hundred there. I didn't ask questions. Just delivered packages. A couple of times I landed in jail for those little envelopes only to be released the next day.

Thinking back, most of it was probably illegal, and I was just hella lucky. I never bothered to check any of the packages. For that reason alone, the Prof trusted me, and I was sucked into the wonderful world of a true fucking idiot. The blinders were on, and I didn't bother to question anything happening around me. The money was great, and the brotherhood took care of me and most of my needs—like providing a place when I wanted to crash somewhere other than home. Food, alcohol and free pussy were always plentiful. As I got older I worked—first odd jobs. A way to get away sometimes, the brotherhood could be suffocating always the talk about killing the niggers, wetbacks, Jews and towelheads. The others thought it was fun to play games, while I only wanted to break-away from those people.

Funny thing, my jobs always had to do with construction. Most building jobs came easy to me; then, a friend introduced me to welding. While apprenticing under a Master Welder and taking classes at Tech school, the money was fucking amazing, and I didn't really use much from my paychecks. I would give my mom the best send off money could buy.

"She didn't want that. A simple cremation was her final wish." My father sobbed, choked up. "She—we decided to spread her ashes on the lake where we used to spend our summers with you in that little town up state. That place reminded her of our hometown in Germany."

I wouldn't argue with my dad. "I understand."

"Make sure everything is done, so you aren't caught in someone else's nonsense. Is this number okay to save? I'll contact you through this."

I glanced at Harper's profile. I didn't think she would mind me using her cell. Temporarily. "Yeah, that's fine. I'll call you tomorrow." I ended the call and held out the phone to return it to Harper.

She didn't immediately take it, and I looked up to find her watching me. Concern was clear in her dark irises. I could lose myself in that look. I held my arms wide open. "I need you."

She closed the gap between us, and the way her sensual form pressed into my body felt so fucking good. Her head to my chest. The way she'd tied her hair back, the locks tickled my chin. I tightened my hold on her. Just being around her forced me to see things differently. I wanted to be someone better and not disappoint the certainty I could see in her eyes. Harper went up on her toes and pressed her lips to mine.

I darted my tongue out to lick her lips. A flavor that was all her own rushed over my taste buds. She opened her mouth and wrapped her tongue around mine. I walked her back until her legs hit the sofa. She dropped, breaking our kiss. I stared down at her, unsure where to start. Tonight, I planned to take my time and worship her body. Tomorrow, I wasn't sure what would happen. I sunk to my knees in front of her.

Slowly, I flicked the button to her jeans free and lowered the zipper. I gripped the waistband of them and yanked, peeling the material down over her ass. She raised her pelvis, and the soft fabric of her panties clung to her hips as I pulled. Harper raised her legs, and I jerked her clothing off, tossing the item over my shoulder. She spread her thighs, and I bowed at the altar that was her pussy.

Under the overhead lights, her juices glistened against her bare folds. I dipped my head. A sweet fruity scent wafted to my nose. I gripped her knees, shoving them farther apart. My fingertips dug into her soft flesh. With my tongue, I lapped at her sweet dew, working my tongue along her sugar coated creases. She swung her legs, bumping my shoulders. I sucked her clit between my lips, rolling it across my tongue, tugging, then relaxing my mouth on the tiny bundle of nerves. Harper pumped her hips, rising off the cushion. She combed her fingers through the strands of my hair, gripping them in tight fists to move my head.

I skimmed my fingers up her thighs and slid two digits into her channel. Deep, garbled moans escaped her. My cock twitched, pushing against the zipper of my jeans. I shuffled my body back to get better access, slamming my fingers into her passage while working her clit in my mouth.

So many senses.

She rolled her pelvis, grinding against my mouth. My heart pounded. A fine sheen of sweat coated my face and neck. I thrust my finger deeper and nipped at her clitoris. High pitched wails filled the air around us. Harper bowed her body, and her knees slammed against my face as she held me in place while her cream spread across my tongue. I eased up, savoring her flavor. My rock hard dick made it uncomfortable to move.

She raised her head and gazed down at me through glazed eyes. This was a simple reminder that I was her man, and I wasn't anywhere near done. I rose and freed the button on my pants, sliding the zipper down. My rod bobbed in freedom. *"Harper."* Her name was my benediction.

A slow smile lifted the corners of her mouth. "I am all yours." She gripped the hem of her t-shirt, snatching it over her head. She undid her bra, freeing the luscious orbs.

I rammed my jeans down my legs and stepped out of them. I claimed a seat beside her. "Ride me, baby."

Tonight was our night, a beginning, because I was never letting her go. We had tomorrow to figure out where we went from here.

30

HARPER

I placed my hands on Dachs shoulders and eased down slowly, ever so slowly upon his thick cock. I watched as it disappeared inside me and didn't stop until I was fully seated on him. When he filled me as far as his length could go, he tightened his hold on my waist,, and we both moaned. I tilted my head back a little and my lips parted.

Jesus, he feels good.

I paused for a moment just enjoying the feel of him surrounding me, the sound of his heavy breathing as he fought not to move yet. That woodsy scent he always seemed to wear that I'd come to associate with him. Then, I opened my eyes and found those ice blue orbs on me. I smiled and pushed up off of him until I paused at his tip before lowering myself down on him again. He leaned forward and captured one of my breasts into his mouth. He tugged on my nipple before circling it with his tongue.

My body quivered, and I could feel the juices pooling from me to coat his dick.

"God, you feel so good," he murmured.

"I need you," I told him.

He released my breasts and moved to cover my mouth with his just as he flexed his thighs rising upward to slam into me. Then he took control of my movement and helped me move up and down on his cock, and I rode him as requested.

I broke away from our kiss; I couldn't breathe; I couldn't get enough air. But, both of our breaths were coming in pants, now. My eyes were closed again as I lost myself in the sensation of feeling full with him inside me, holding me, completing me. I could feel the sweat covering my skin, I could feel the same on his arms, wherever I touched. But, the sound of our lovemaking, the moans, the air leaving our lungs, our bodies colliding is what I focused on most—the ultimate pleasure, the sensations. Dachs took us to a height I'd never visited before and didn't want to leave.

Our movements became faster, our breathing harsher; we were both covered in sweat now and were so close to that oblivion. He was holding back but so was I, holding on to this feeling for as long as I could, this joining of our bodies. Finally, we could stem this avalanche no longer, he groaned as his body jerked. My core clenched at the same time and together we soared over the edge.

As our bodies joined, so did our juices. We kept moving even after we were both spent, milking every last drop. We stilled, and our racing hearts slowed. I opened my eyes, and he smiled just before he kissed me again. This one long and deep as our tongues joined once more.

"Wrap your legs around me," he said.

I did and lay my head against his shoulder. I could feel his cock soften and as he stood he slid out of me, but I didn't mind. He walked us to my bedroom and lay me down on the bed, coming down beside me. I pulled the covers over our naked bodies, wrapped in his arms, and fully satisfied; I fell asleep.

I OPENED my eyes to the morning light and smiled. I could feel Dachs lips against the side of my neck. His strong arms still around me. Without turning around I said, "It's about time I woke up with you in my bed." I didn't see it but I could feel his smile.

He turned me over until I lay on my side, facing him. The smile I sensed was plastered on his face, but there was a touch of sadness in his eyes. It hadn't been there last night as we made love, but I suspected there would be times when its presence would be there. My baby had been through a lot, and it wasn't exactly over. But, I would do what I can to keep that sadness away.

"Good morning, beautiful," he said.

I smiled. "Morning, handsome. Are you going to make this a habit?"

He held onto one of my locks and twirled it around his finger, something he'd done last night too. "Maybe. If you want me too."

I couldn't seem to stop smiling as I leaned forward and gave him a quick kiss.

We were both just staring at each other and grinning like a couple of idiots but it felt so good.

"I've got to get up and go. I've got to go home, take a shower and get to class, then work," he finally said. "I was waiting for you to wake up, with a little help." He winked.

I knew he was in a technical school and was pretty proud of him. I'd always known there was more to him than his damn tats. My gaze moved to the HH on the side of his neck, and I leaned forward and licked it. "You know I now claim these as mine. We were destined to be."

He chuckled. "I'll take your word for it." Dachs sat up and

hesitated, glancing down to meet my gaze. "My life changed when this little persistence black girl decided to sit near me."

"That's right and what I say goes."

"Do you have class today?" he asked.

"No, tomorrow. Are you sure about going to class today?"

"I'll be fine. It's what my mom would want me to do. I've got a test today. But, maybe I won't go to work. I'll see if I can trade shifts with a friend. I need to go see my dad. I'll do that after class. Come with me. I want him to meet you."

"Are you sure it's the right time?"

"No time like the present. I'll come meet you after class about 11:00, and then, we can take the T."

"Ah, that's fine but I can drive."

He chuckled again. I loved to hear even that small note of joy from him.

"Let me guess." He stared at me for a minute. "A Mercedes."

I sat up and punched his arm. "No, BMW."

His laughter deepened. "So, why was it every time I saw you you were either taking the T or Uber?"

"Why do you think?"

He frowned then smiled. "You're a stalker."

"It worked."

He pulled me to him and kissed me again. "I really want to keep doing that, but if I do we might never get out of bed."

"And that's bad..."

"I need to get my Master Welder's Certification to make more money. I'm sure my savings is only enough for the retainer of that lawyer you hired for me. I also need to help my dad rebuild the shop...now that Mom is gone." He combed his fingers through his hair.

That sobered me up. I placed my hand on his face. "I'm sorry, babe, so sorry about your mom."

"I know." He covered my hand with his palm. "Thanks."

I took a deep breath. I'd planned on paying for Donald's services. He was one of the best and didn't come cheap and I knew Dachs would never be able to have access to someone like Donald, but there was one thing I knew about my Dachs. Well, maybe two things, one he was mine, and two, he had his pride. "I'll make sure Donald gives you a discount."

"Don't worry about it. He and I already discussed his fees."

"Really, what's he charging you?"

"He's giving me a flat rate, but even as expensive as it is, he's still giving me something off, and I need him."

"Okay, good."

He rose from the bed and stretched. His back was too me, and damn if I didn't lick my lips at the sight of all that sleek muscle before me. I itched to get him back into bed, so I could trace all those nooks and crannies with my tongue. But then, he turned around. He was sporting a semi and as my eyes were riveted on his cock, it jerked.

"Don't look at me like that."

I placed one hand under my head and shifted the covers so he could see my body. "Like what?" I asked all wide eyed and innocent like.

"That. That right there." He began to back out of the room since his clothes were all out in the other room, where we'd left them last night. "I'll be back about 11:00 to take you home."

"And, I'm driving."

"Sure, whatever."

Then, he rushed out of the room as I laughed because now, he was wearing a full on woody.

"That's gotta hurt," I yelled after him.

"I'll live," he yelled back.

31

DACHS

I couldn't focus on class. My project for final certification was basically done; all I had to do was make it pretty for the professor who loved aesthetics. One by one, I yanked my fingers free from the gloves and tossed them down beside me. I stared up at the bookshelf, seven foot high by four foot wide; it was meant to be an industrial piece created with steel and fire. Once powder-coated, it would look like any other furniture piece meant strictly for function. I skimmed my palms across the joints, smooth as a baby's bottom. A snort escaped me; I am good at what I know. Still, something was missing—my own special touch.

I reached beneath my apron and dug my cell free from my jean's pocket. There were still a couple hours before I met Harper. I set my phone on a shelf and squatted to go through the wire and metal scraps.

She claimed my HH tattoo as her own, I would make it so. Laying out the spare pieces in front of me, I created a design integrating the letters and using the last of a roll of thin wire, I sculpted a small flower connecting the harsh lines. I lifted my gloves to put them on.

"What are you up too, Mr. Neumann?" My teacher, and Master welder, stopped beside me. She held a clipboard in her hands.

"Besides paint, this looks like a finished piece."

Of course, it did. I already knew my job, understood the craft. All I needed was the actual certificate. In the past I would ignore her. The woman clearly wasn't white. Her brown skin and tight curls could have been a mix of many ethnicities. Not so long ago her very existence was against my principles. I straightened and peered down at the much shorter woman. It was the first time I'd ever really looked at her. There was a kindness in her features I'd never noticed; a hint of a smile lifted the corners of her mouth.

"I was thinking of adding a little something extra. Just because it's functional furniture doesn't mean it can't be pretty." Lord, I said those words out loud. I sucked in a deep breath, prepared for the laughter I was sure would come—the ridicule of making something seemingly more feminine.

"Well, there are quite a few women in the industry now." She nodded. "I can attest to that."

No mockery. The more I learned about other races, the stronger my realization that I was a fool. I wasted so many damn years. A deep exhale blew through my mouth.

"It's your final project and twenty-five percent of your grade. You already completed your apprenticeship. Mr. Neumann, I do believe you did things a bit backwards." A soft chuckle erupted from her. "I look forward to seeing your final piece." She scribbled something on her notepad and ambled away.

It seemed I was always doing things a bit off. I grabbed my cell to check the time. There was no time to finish; I would have to complete the shelf in a few days. As long as the project was turned in on time, then there would be no worries. I cleared my workspace and locked my tools away. Harper was waiting for me.

WE SAT IN HER CAR, staring at the boarded up picture window of my family's pierogi shop. Soot covered the once pristine bricks of the storefront. My mother took pride in our place of business. Thankfully the fire didn't make it past the entrance and the damage looked worse than it actually was. Mostly cosmetic, the water did more harm to the building than the fire.

Because my mother took the brunt of the Molotov Cocktail.

I know I needed to move, open the door, get out the car, but that day was playing on a loop in my head and left me incapacitated.

A gentle touch on my hand took me out of my headspace and claimed my attention. I glanced down to find Harper's hand covering mine. I followed the length of her arm up to her face with my gaze.

She freed her hand and cupped my jaw. "Are you alright?"

I would never be alright. I could only get used to my new normal. "I'm fine."

"You don't look fine." She narrowed her eyes and cocked her head, her dreads brushing her shoulder.

I opened my mouth to speak when there was a knock on my window. I twisted to find my dad staring at us through the glass. His eyes wide, he held his hand up mid-knock. I motioned for him to move and opened the door. Harper opened hers at the same time.

"You have been down here a long time. I wasn't sure if it was you..." My dad's gaze kept drifting to Harper. "You brought company?"

There was no need to hide my relationship with Harper. "She is my girlfriend." It was hard to control the hint of a smile sending the corners of my mouth upward. The tension in his shoulders eased. It felt good to say those words out loud.

My dad was quiet for a long time. He leaned into me. "Son, I thought you—ah—she is..."

"It's a pleasure to meet you, Mr. Neumann." Harper held out her hand to my father.

He took it, warmly covering her palm with both hands. "It is mine, the pleasure." There was just a hint of Eastern European accent to my dad's words. "Come up. I have lunch waiting." He moved away toward the alley.

I took Harper's hand and followed my old man to the entrance to the upper apartment. On the landing that led to the second floor the scent of smoke lingered in the air. Peering through the doorway that led to the kitchen, the room was immaculate as always. I navigated the narrow stairway, pulling Harper behind me.

In the apartment, the kitchen table was laden with food. "Sit down." My dad waved his hands down, motioning toward the seats. "It has been a long time since Dachs has sat at this table." A thread of sadness was clear in his tone.

"He's here now." Harper inserted a vein of cheerfulness into her voice.

"I'm sorry." I didn't know what else to say. I wasn't sure how to maintain my relationship with my father with both of us knowing I was the reason my mother was dead.

"He is." As if speaking to the room in general. "Mama would be happy." My dad sighed as he took a seat.

"I can help with the funeral." I awkwardly blurted out before dropping into a chair. I know my father wouldn't accept my help, but I had to try one more time.

"No need. Arrangements were made a long time ago for both your mother and me. Eat." My dad pushed a dish in mine and Harper's direction. "And, tell me how you two met."

For the first time since all the bullshit started, I saw my father smile.

32

HARPER

The wind tried to whip my locks around, but I had them braided together so it was a losing battle. Instead, the chill seeped through my coat, and I shivered. Dachs wrapped his arm around me as I stood at the edge of the lake beside him and his father. We were saying goodbye to the woman who'd borne him. They flung her ashes into the wind and it picked up the remains, carrying it over the water. As the sunlight hit the particles, they sparkled with warmth. Still, I felt the pain of both men as I held Dachs waist. I regretted that I'd never get to meet this woman. I wanted to tell her 'thank you.' At his core, Dachs was a good person, and that was his mother's doing. He'd told me that more than once, so did his father.

That day Dachs took me home with him to meet his father was very healing for them both. I know his father was both shocked and pleased to see me, a person of another race by his son's side. His smiles were warm and welcoming. When he'd asked how we'd met Dachs said, "She stalked me."

I lightly slapped his arm. "Okay, well kinda, we kinda stalked each other."

His father chuckled.

"That's true, until I wore her down," Dachs said, squeezing my hand.

His father told stories of Dachs when he was younger, even pulling out the baby pictures. I laughed to see the naked two-year-old, blond-haired boy hugging his mother and smiling as he pulled her into the tub. Dachs was the splitting image of his mother with her eyes. Both Dachs and his father laughed too at the memories. I felt I got a glimpse at the woman who'd raised him and the man who'd fathered him. In the end, Dachs had been true to who he was. His father had forgiven him, and hopefully with my help, Dachs would forgive himself and move forward.

Hand in hand we walked back to the cars. His dad had driven up separately from us. Dachs and I would head back to Boston right now, but his dad would stay in the small town for the night. Dachs drove my car the two hour trip back since I'd driven us out. He was quiet on the return drive, but it wasn't uncomfortable. He kept our fingers entwined and every so often, he'd rub his thumb against my palm. When he did speak, it was about his mom and me.

"I should have done a lot of things differently," he said. "Mom would have liked you. I'm sorry she never got a chance to meet you." He raised my hand and kissed my knuckles. "No. She would have loved you."

It was on the tip of my tongue to tell him I would have loved her too as I loved her son. But I didn't. I was sure Dachs loved me, but it was something he had to figure out for himself. If he didn't and soon...well, I'd just have to tell him. For now, I replied, "I know I would have loved her too. I adore your dad. You're a lot like him."

"I'm not nearly the man he is, but I'll get there. They both hated that I was part of NMAWP."

Dachs didn't refer to the men and women as the brotherhood or the members as his brothers and sisters any more—kinda hard to do when they killed your mother and then, tried to blame it on you. "But, you're out of all of that now, and the police are gathering up all the members involved."

"They've found everyone, except Bruno."

"Still no word on him?"

"None. I don't want to think about him or them right now." He glanced at me and smiled. "I want to think about you—about us."

"So, I'm your girlfriend?" I asked. It didn't escape my notice how he'd introduced me to his dad.

"Yes."

"And, so we're clear, you are my boyfriend." It wasn't a question and by his grin, he knew it.

"Yes."

"Good. Are you...are you at all worried?"

"Hell no. Let any of those fuckers come for me or you. You're mine."

I smiled. "Goes both ways, babe. No one better mess with you either."

It was his turn to smile. "Tell me about your dad."

One reason we were headed back sooner was to have dinner with my dad later tonight. "Are you scared to meet him?"

"Not really."

I chuckled. "Don't worry, my dad is a fair man. He will treat you as you treat him. As long as you respect me and make me happy, he'll be happy."

He glanced at me. "Are you happy?"

"What do you think?"

"Like I told my dad, I think you stalked me enough to wear me down. But I'm not complaining. If that's what makes you happy...I should do my part to make sure you are satisfied and don't go stalking anyone else." He glanced at me and winked.

"I got what I wanted." And, I did. I guess I'd always been spoiled like that.

"Do you always get your way?"

"Are you reading my mind? With you, I better."

"What have you told him about me?"

I'd thought about that long and hard, what to tell my dad. But, he and I never lied to each other. Besides, my father was well informed, and I'm sure he already got phone calls from his lawyer as well as the chief of police about my involvement with Dachs. So, when I'd called him to tell him I had someone I wanted him to meet—he already knew. I told him everything. Well, everything he needed to know. Was he happy about it? Not at first. But I reminded him about the woman he married and how I felt about that, and he shut up. I've been nothing but respectful to Teresa. I expected the same consideration from my father. To at least give my choice a chance.

"Everything," I said to Dachs.

He looked a bit uneasy but then nodded. "I've made mistakes. They won't happen again. Is he going to have a problem with the fact that I can't give you the kind of things you are accustomed to? At least, not yet."

"Hey, hey, hey. If I wanted a man to give me anything, I would not be working my ass off in college and trying to get an internship to lead to a great job. If I want something, I can damn well buy it myself."

"Still..."

I shook my head. "No stills, ands, ifs, or buts about it. Get that through your thick head." I squeezed his hand. "You know I'm always right."

"I'll let you keep thinking that." He chuckled.

We made good time getting back to the city. When we

walked into the restaurant, we were immediately shown to the table where my father was already seated. He was alone, which I was thankful for. I wasn't sure if Teresa would be joining us and was happy she wasn't. I wanted this first meeting to just be between us.

I knew Dachs was nervous by the tight grip he had on my hand under the table, but outwardly it didn't show. All in all, the first few minutes went well, until after we ordered. Then dad sat back and the grilling began.

"So, you're a neo-Nazi?"

"I was. Not now, though...Sir."

My father asked the hard questions but Dachs made no excuses and held his own.

I knew my dad was somewhat mollified because Dachs was helping to put the bastards in jail.

"I'm sorry about your mother," Dad said.

"Thank you."

"We released her ashes today," I said.

"Why didn't you let me know? We could have done this another time."

"It's fine," Dachs said. "I wanted to meet you. Harper is important to me, and I wanted you to know that."

"Good. She's the most important person in my life."

"Dad." I reached across the table and held his hand, giving it a good squeeze before releasing him. I'd always known that, but it was always nice to hear it.

Dinner arrived but still my dad peppered Dachs with questions about school, his job, what he expected to do after he was finished, and without pause, Dachs answered everyone.

I couldn't be more proud of him. We were just about to order dessert when Dachs' phone beeped.

"I'm sorry, I have to take this." He got up and walked out to the lobby.

I leaned forward and said to my dad, "Well. Did he pass?"

My father flinched. "Can he do something about that tattoo? When your stepmother sees that..."

"You have tattoos," I reminded him. He had one on his ankle: a rose, my mother's favorite flower, something Teresa didn't know and I wasn't about to tell her, and a Celtic band on his bicep.

"Well yeah, but neither of mine have anything to do with hate."

"Well that HH on his neck happens to stand for Harper Hodges." That was my story and I was sticking to it.

My father cracked up.

"Sorry."

I glanced up as Dachs slid back into the seat next to mine.

"That was Donald. They have Bruno in custody, and he wants me down at the police station first thing tomorrow."

33

DACHS

I arrived at the police station lobby earlier than I'd intended. My lawyer hadn't arrived yet and I paced the small area, an uncomfortable feeling slithering down my spine. My gut roiled. I learned a long time ago to listen to my body, something was about to happen I just wasn't sure what. Time slowed and the ticks of the clock above an interior door felt way too long.

That door opened and a detective, the old black guy, slipped through the opening. What was his name? I racked my brain for the answer and realized I didn't know it. The last time we clashed I was too busy trying to clear my name to worry about his. I guess he could read the look on my face. The cop didn't offer his hand, but he did utter his name.

"I'm Detective Benson." He pushed the barrier wider. "There are a few questions that need clearing up. We can do that at my desk."

I followed, cautiously. My trust for the authorities was still questionable and my lawyer wasn't there to back me up. Our footfalls echoed through the empty hallway. I glanced around, watching the closed doors as we passed them. Behind one of them was Bruno's punk ass. I didn't care how long it would take but once I settled up with Bruno, I might be able to put the situation behind me. Beating his ass to a bloody pulp would go a long way to making me feel better. If I could get to the Prof, I would gladly do the time I was given to beat his ass again too.

At the intersection where one passageway met the one I traveled; officers accompanied another man. I peered at the person as he passed me. A cuffed Bruno. I did pride myself on a fair fight. It just wasn't going to happen today. I balled my hand into a fist at my side. The smirk on Bruno's face when he gazed over at me. Our stares locked and the fucker blew me a kiss. Yeah, there was nothing, and no one that would stop me from whooping his ass. In the enclosed passage it wasn't hard to break past the policemen flanking him. My fist connected with his ribs in a solid blow. Caught off guard, Bruno reeled back and slammed into the wall. He swung his arms up and I dodged the blow, retaliating with a knee to his ribcage. Bruno tried to block my punches, bending his arms in front of him to protect his upper body and face. Cops yelled around us then blessed silence.

"Not today, you son of a bitch." I growled and plowed my fist into his gut. "My mother, you fucking bastard. My mother!" Words fell from my lips like lodestones.

His grunts, painful sounding wails, eclipsed my sentences. The only sounds came from us.

Squeaks from someone's shoes on the linoleum, flesh pounding into flesh no one was stopping me. I owed the sadistic bastard for Harper, for my mom, for me.

I rammed a knee into his thigh and the asshole's leg buckled. That was the only window I needed. In steel toe work boots, I jammed my foot into anywhere on his body I could reach. Bruno sank lower to the floor, and I gave less than a fuck where my kicks landed. He shifted to all fours and moved to crawl.

"Where the hell you going?" I slammed my boot into his cheek.

His head twisted and blood flew from his mouth to splatter the wall. It wasn't enough. I needed more retribution. I aimed for his head again. He rose up on his knees and covered his face with his arms.

"No!" Bruno cried out. "Stop!"

In our organization taking a punch or a kick was a necessity. How many times had we jumped in boys so much younger than us that didn't utter a sound, and this punk ass bitch was begging? Did my mom get a chance to ask for her life? I lowered my foot and crouched down to meet him eye to eye. Tears rolled down his cheeks. A rivulet of blood trickled from the corner of his lip. My heart pounded in my chest. Sweat dotted my face. I cocked my head and stared at him. In truth, I was no better than the bastard before me; I was as dirty as he was—dirtier because I couldn't even claim I was a psychopath. I took no joy in what I did over the years, I simply thought it was the right thing to do. Keep the races separate. I lost so many years believing the bullshit. I exhaled and rose up then I threw my head back and screamed, pouring out all the anguish of my time lost. And, just as suddenly, I stopped.

I was tapped on the shoulder, and I glanced back to see Benson standing behind me.

"You finished?" The old man gazed at me without blinking. "Got it all out?"

What could I say? Whooping Bruno's ass would never be enough, but it was a good start. "Yeah." I snorted.

"Good. You are under arrest." Benson held up a pair of cuffs.

It wasn't lost on me that I was given time to beat Bruno's ass. I guess I had the old, black detective to thank for that. Harper was going to be pissed, and my lawyer, well, I just added to his caseload.

I held my arms together behind my back. "Thank you." I muttered.

"I didn't do it for you. I did it for the nice woman that by all accounts did not deserve what she suffered." Benson continued reading me my Miranda rights. He chuckled "And, I get to throw your ass in jail for a bit." He yanked me back.

"Aren't I the lucky one," I countered dryly, shuffling my feet."

Cops squeezed past me and helped Bruno up. The fucker slumped between the policemen and was walked/dragged away from me down the hall. I took a step forward, my anger still palatable.

"Don't make me pepper spray you," Benson sighed. "For a minute there, you were kinda growing on me."

"You say the nicest things." I meant it. Benson was growing on me too.

"Guess we are never too late to learn a little something." He swung me around and walked me in the opposite direction of where Bruno was taken. "No use looking back. That boy on his way to infirmary. I do believe you broke some of his ribs." He paused. "Now I got to figure out how to write this bullshit up."

"Blame it on the steel toe boots. A lot of damage in a little time." I was trying to help him out by tossing out excuses.

"I just might do that." Our conversation ended when I was handed over to an officer to be placed in a holding cell.

The cell was blessedly empty, and I cried like a baby, for all that I lost. Still, I knew what I was doing when I did it, and I would accept the consequences for my actions. The burn building in my chest was my repentance.

EPILOGUE

The stadium was filled to capacity. No matter what direction I looked there was a sea of faces all staring down at the stage. They were all different colors. It took some getting used to, reminding myself that one race was no better than the other. I sat between my dad and Harper's dad and beside him, his wife. Her dad made light conversation in generalities. I knew I still made him a little uncomfortable, but it was a start. My father would lean across me easily chatting with Harper's pops. Her stepmother flat out refused to talk to me and would instead offer sly, curious glances my way whenever we were together. It would be so much easier if the woman would just ask her questions. I had no problem giving her an honest answer. Instead, she would just roll her eyes in my direction. It wasn't my first time dealing with ignorant people. It was more important to keep the peace. Harper and I, we had plans. I received my certification, and with her getting her degree, we decided to start fresh. She wanted to move to New York, and I wanted to move to Chicago. We flipped a coin. I won. In a few weeks we would make the move. We both already had job offers.

I gazed down at the floor, searching for Harper. It was impossible to recognize her amongst the yards of black fabric and square caps.

Her father leaned over, bumping my shoulder. "I haven't heard anything else. Have the court dates been set?"

It was almost impossible to hear him over the din of chatter going on around us. I twisted in my seat to face him. "Sorry, I missed what you said." I glanced past him to find his wife tinkering with her cell. Yet, she leaned in our direction.

"I asked how your case was going. I heard there was a small issue, then nothing."

I smiled at her dad. "It was nothing serious and easily handled. I completed my community service. Now, we are just waiting for the dates for Bruno and Dwight." I spoke up to be heard. I might have to do quite a bit of commuting to attend the trials, but that would just give me another excuse to stay with my dad, especially, since he decided to reopen the pierogi shop and run it by himself. I understood where my father was coming from. The most time he'd spent with my mother was in that shop they built together. It wouldn't be fair to ask him to leave it.

Overhead lights dimmed and spotlights illuminated the stage. The din of chatter quieted. Educators were announced and marched up, taking their seats while the orator claimed a spot behind the podium. Images replaced the blue screen over the stage.

"My little girl is graduating." Harper's father stared ahead, a bright grin on his face. He nodded. Pride rolled off of him in waves.

Introductions were made, and names were called. Screams from different parts of the arena could be heard as each student walked across the stage, then accepted the documents being thrust into their hands. When Harper's turn came, I stood, stomped and yelled. My dad patted my arm. I was drawing attention to myself and gave less than a damn. Harper was my woman, and I would do whatever was needed to support her. We had a long road ahead of us but I believed—truly believed—together there would be nothing we couldn't accomplish.

I left my seat, pushing past the throngs of people who'd been seated alongside me. Bumping knees, tossing out *'sorry'* as I moved. In that instant I wanted to see Harper and not on the mega screen hung over the stage. I needed to touch, to speak to her. Tell her for the millionth time how proud I was of her. I ran to the narrow stairway, rushing to get to the main floor. Crowds filled the doorways, and I shoved my way through them. Moving past each section, inching closer to the stage, searching for Harper. Did I miss her? Had she returned to her seat? I caught sight of her laughing with friends. She took their hands and gave gentle shakes before moving away from them. I moved parallel to her, catching her at the end of a row.

She gazed up at me through wide eyes, and I caught her up in my arms, lifting her above me. "I love you," I uttered against her cheek.

Harper shook her head and motioned toward her ears, the envelope in her hand brushing her face.

I lowered her, sliding her body against mine. I leaned in, my lips brushing the shell of her ear. "I. Love. You."

She reared back and gazed into my eyes. Hers were bright with unshed tears, yet a beaming smile graced her features. Harper dropped the envelope, clutched my face between her palms, and pressed her mouth against mine.

I felt her lips as they moved, her breath blowing into my mouth as she spoke. "I love you too."

This woman belonged with me. No matter the circumstances I truly believed together, there was nothing we couldn't withstand.

The End
Thanks for reading!

Keep reading for a sneak peek at
Quiet Strength
Serena & Gage's story
Coming Soon

CHAPTER 1

SERENA

I'd known the parade in honor of Dr. Martin Luther King might have gotten rowdy, especially the counter one in protest of his work. I'd anticipated yelling, screaming, maybe a few fights even. The cops were positioned all along the street, the roads had been blocked off with police vehicles, and I even saw a tank, so no cars could crash into the crowds. But I never anticipated frigging bombs.

The White Nationalist Party, the fucktards, had hosted a counter parade a couple blocks over from the city sponsored parade in honor of Dr. King. So much for a peaceful march my ass, those people tossed Molotov Cocktails into the crowd lining the sidewalk to 'boo' them. As I stood on the sidewalk with my friends, an explosion, then another right after, rocked around us. One of those things went off not far from where I stood with my friends. Then all hell broke loose.

I was thankful I wasn't in the direct path of it, none of us were. Yet debris flew everywhere and a piece managed to clip my head and it was lights out for me. Of the five of us, I was the only one just close enough to get knocked out. When I came too again, I was in the hospital and my best friends, Harper and

        Chapter 1

James were hovering around me. He had a white bandage wrapped around his left hand.

"Wha...what happened?" I asked Harper as I raised my hand to my head. I could feel a bandage just over my right eye.

"A part of a sign or something hit you on the head. Do you remember the parade?"

"Yeah, the explosions. Then something hit me."

"There's a bandage over your eye; you have a cut there hopefully it won't scar, but it's right on your eyebrow. Even if it scars you can always fill it in," Harper told me and squeezed my hand.

"Wow, I only remember getting hit in the head then nothing til now."

"At first, we thought it was your eye, because of all the blood, but it's not," James added.

"Thank God," I said.

"You also have a few cuts from the glass on your neck but nothing serious; they shouldn't scar either," Harper added.

I touched my neck, happy to hear that. I glanced at James' hand. "What happened to your hand?"

James held up his hand for me to see. "Nothing too serious; it's a good thing it's my left hand though since I'm right-handed. I got a few cuts from the glass blasting onto the sidewalk. I'd raised my hands to protect myself. I hadn't even realized they were cut up until we got to the hospital."

Before I could ask any more questions another person entered the room.

"Good, you're awake. I'm Dr Malberry. How are you feeling?"

A man in a white coat came over to the bed and Harper stepped aside.

"Like, I have a headache," I told him.

"No surprise. Give us a moment, and let me get a look at your friend," the doctor told Harper and James.

My friends stepped out of the room as the doctor examined

me. Apparently, they'd already taken me to do a CAT scan, and it was all good. Thank Christ it looked like I just suffered a mild concussion and had a cut over my eye that only needed one of those dissolvable stitches.

After the doctor let Harper and James back, the first thing Harper said was, "Your parents are on their way. They'll be here shortly."

"Crap." My parents were worry warts. I was their only girl and not supposed to be in danger, unlike my brother who was on a nuclear sub somewhere in some ocean he couldn't say. We only spoke to him about every three months.

"You were unconscious, and your mom called me as soon as we got to the hospital," Harper said. "She'd been watching the news, and the explosion was all over it. She knew we'd planned on coming down for the parade and wanted to make sure we weren't with the protestors. I had to tell her we were and that you got hurt."

"Yeah, I know. It's fine. So, is it only the cuts to your hands?" I asked James. "And how about you, Harper and everyone else?"

"Just this," James said. "My dad should be here any second now too; he saw the news and already spoke to me. And everyone else is fine. They came to the hospital but this place is a madhouse, they had to leave. They'd only let the two of us in here with you."

"And I'm fine. Not a scratch. But, you gave us quite a scare," Harper told me and hugged me just as James' phone dinged.

"That's my dad; he's looking for me. I'm glad you're going to be okay. If you need anything just call but I'll check on you later."

James wrapped his arms around Harper then me and left us both. The doctor came in right after and told me he looked over all of my results, and he would sign the paperwork to release me, but my activities would be restricted for the next twenty-four hours.

Harper looked at me and grinned. She left me to go get a soda while I waited for my release papers and my parents. I heard my mother's voice in the hallway before I saw them.

They rushed to my bedside, and I was happy to see them. "I'm fine, parents." Was the first thing I said to them before they could get a word in, I knew it's what they wanted to know. I sat up and grinned at them both. "The doctor's already released me."

"Thank God! You could have been seriously hurt," my mom said. "But she wasn't," my dad offered as he kissed my forehead. "Our baby girl's going to be alright."

"Okay, but what did the doctor say? What happened?" my mom asked as she touched the bandage over my eye.

I told them.

"Sweet Jesus," my mother cried and hugged me again. "You're sure you feel fine? And, how about Harper and the others?"

"James' hand got cuts from broken glass, but Harper's fine. She'll be right back. And I just have to take it easy, no exercise or anything strenuous for the next day or so. I don't even have to take any meds."

"What about Steve," my mom asked.

"He wasn't with us, he's out of town for a few days."

"Okay, you ready to go then?" my dad asked. "We can go to your place and get your things. Your mom already has us booked into a hotel. We'll take care of you and make sure you are all good before we leave in a couple of days."

I groaned.

"We leave after we speak to the doctor," my mom added.

"That's fine. You can take me home, but I'm not staying at the hotel with you. I will be fine back at my apartment. You can check on me there."

"We'll see what the doctor says, specially since your roommate wouldn't be there," my mother added.

"He wouldn't be there anyway since he has to work." I'd sigh but it would do no good. If the doctor told them I shouldn't be alone, they wouldn't bother taking me to the apartment I shared with a roommate. They'd take me to whatever hotel they were staying in. I couldn't have that. If push came to shove, and I insisted on staying in my apartment, which I would, I know my mom would stay on the pull out couch.

"Do you have all of your things?" my mother asked.

"Yes, but we can't leave yet anyway, Harper went to get a soda, and she left her bag here. Let me go get her," I said.

"No, tell me where she is and I'll go find her," my dad offered.

"It's fine. I'm fine, promise." I stood. "I want to get a drink of water too and just want to stretch my legs. Besides, I can see the doctor at the nurse's station, better grab him while you can. I'll be right back with Harper."

I hurried out of the room before they could protest. I loved my parents, but they could be just a tad too much at times. Besides, I'd heard the nurses talking about how some of the skin heads had gotten attacked and were in the hospital too and no one wanted to treat them. I can't say I blamed them, nor did I want my father to run into any of them. My dad was in special forces until a flash bomb went off too close to his eyes. He could see, but he had to wear some heavy duty glasses, so he got a medical discharge. He did consulting and training for the private sector now. So, my father running into any Nazis' Neo or otherwise, right now, might not end well at all.

But, I was more worried about Harper; she'd been gone a little too long, and she was dating one of them. I still had a hard time wrapping my head around the fact that my black upper class, totally left bougie in the dust, friend was seeing a skinhead. I hoped for her sake, he had nothing to do with that bomb. I needed to make sure she was alright. A nurse had also mentioned someone had died.

I didn't want to stop at the nurse's station because the doctor still stood there, and my parents were headed in that direction. I spied an elevator and moved toward it. There was a sign next to the call buttons that said beverage and snack machines on the 4th floor, that was two floors up. I pressed the elevator button, and as I waited, I sent a text to Harper to let her know my parents had arrived.

The minute the elevator doors opened, and I stepped out I knew I'd made a mistake. There were those white shirts, red suspenders, black pants wearing assholes everywhere on that floor. The same clothes they wore during the march. I wanted so badly to get back on the elevator and return to the safety of my parents, but I had to make sure Harper wasn't anywhere near this mess. I glanced away from the five men congregated at one end of the hall and looked in the other direction. I could see the edges of the soda machines, so I moved that way. As I did my phone buzzed with a text. It was from Harper she was headed back to my room. I breathed a sigh of relief and turned sharply back in the direction of the elevator when I ran into something solid as a rock.

Red filled my vision—red suspenders. I tilted my head back and looked up into the piercing amber eyes of my enemy. We stared silently at each other for I don't know how long. No one else existed for me in that hallway at that moment. I could feel the blood pumping through my heart, pushing through my veins, readying me to fight or flight, but as we stared mutely at each other, something unspoken passed between us. Without taking my gaze from his, I reached over and pressed the elevator button. It was still on the floor, so the doors opened immediately. He didn't move except for the flaring of his nostrils. Without turning my back to him, I got on the elevator and pressed my floor. The doors seemed to slowly close as we continued to silently stare at each other.

Not until the elevator began to move did I release the breath I'd been holding.

What the hell?

CHAPTER 2

GAGE

I couldn't stop looking at her. No, not a *her—an it*. Her very being should have been an affront to my senses. Still, I couldn't look away until the damn doors closed, literally breaking our connection. A link that should not exist.

I stared at my image in the polished metal doors, but it wasn't me that I saw. It was the niggeress with her creamy chocolate skin, hair pulled back into a ponytail giving her features an exotic look, making her thick lips...I shook my head. Those thoughts, I couldn't let them continue down that path in my mind. I abruptly backed up and spun around to walk down the hall. The medicinal smell wafting through the passage made my head hurt. Dealing with Dwight added to my stress.

My dad's younger half-brother, the Professor as he had built himself up to be was walking a knive's edge with authorities and his sanity had become seriously questionable. Sent at my father's request to not only bring supplies for the parade but also to check on Dwight. I stopped at a wall of windows in a small waiting area, someplace quiet and dug the cell from my pocket. A few stabs with my finger on the screen and rings could be heard through the tiny earpiece.

"Son." My Pop's gruff tone filled my ear.

I stared down into the tree dotted parking lot that looked more like a park with it wrought iron benches and colorful foliage. "Dwight is a problem." Even though he is a blood relative I found it hard to work up any respect for the man.

"Can you clean up the mess this time?"

That was dad. Straight to the point. I followed the various people walking to their vehicles with my sight. I found myself tracking the niggers crossing the concrete slabs. "Not this time. Someone died. Dachs mother. I think good ole Dwight did it on purpose."

"The fuck!" Dad's voice exploded through the earpiece. "That dumb son of a-"

"Careful, you're talking about grandma." I couldn't hide the chuckle threatening to burst past my lips." Grandma raised both boys and my aunt with distinctive beliefs. Each of grandma's children have a different father. Something about the disappointment of men and hell, I just tuned the old woman out after a while.

"It's her fault I am stuck taking care of the little shit and the reason you are always having to clean up his bullshit."

Dad has a point. Nothing could save grandma's youngest from his latest stupidity. Wait until Aunt Grace got a whiff of what happened. As an elected official no one knew her true values and she sometimes used her position for—well—more than expected. Looked like her brother was going to sink any further aspirations she may have in climbing the political office ladder, if the word got out of who he really was. "Dachs-"

Dad cut me off. "That boy is a damn good soldier for our cause. To alienate one of our own. That fucking asshole."

Good soldier alright. Not the way Dachs was watching that porch monkey. His brother had a bad case of jungle fever. *The way you watched that niggeress. Are you any different?*

REVIEWS

Thank you for reading. If you enjoyed this work or any others, please leave a review. Without you our writing is just words on a page.

MEANWHILE

While you wait for Quiet Strength check out the latest from Ursula's alter ego, LaVerne Thompson as well as Kassanna.

Sometimes running is not the answer. Then again, when your life is on the line, sometimes it can be.
An Action Adventure Urban Fantasy

https://books2read.com/u/4XQwa5

———————

From Kassanna

Available on Amazon

ABOUT THE AUTHORS

Ursula Sinclair is the alter ego of LaVerne Thompson a USA Today Bestselling, award winning, multi-published author, an avid reader and a writer of contemporary, fantasy, and sci/fi sensual romances. She loves creating worlds within and without our world. She writes romantic suspense and new adult romance under the pen name Ursula Sinclair.

She is a certified chocoholic and is currently working on several projects. Some might even involve chocolate. But, writing helps maintain her sanity.

Sign up for her newsletter for sneak peeks and advance info on new releases as well as a few freebies to subscribers. http://bit.ly/1hA7C9W

Read More from Ursula Sinclair

WWW.URSULASINCLAIR.COM OR WWW.LAVERNETHOMPSON.COM

MORE ABOUT THE AUTHORS

Kassanna is a strong believer in love at first sight and happily ever after.

Writing has always been her passion, but fate sometimes has other roads that must first be taken. Navigating the road less traveled was not only unexpected, but in the end, extremely rewarding. Her books are mainly contemporary romance, but she has delved into the paranormal, fantasy, and plans on expanding into other areas as the ideas come to her. Right now, she is enjoying life and seeing her works come into fruition, making it that much more pleasurable especially when her books make others smile. Kassanna wouldn't have it any other way.

http://www.flavorfullove.com

OTHER BOOKS BY LAVERNE THOMPSON/URSULA SINCLAIR

PARANOMAL/ROMANTIC FANTASY/URBAN FANTASY

SERIES

Story of the Brethren

A romantic fantasy

Dragon's Heart Book 1

Dragon's Blood Book 2

Redemption

An urban fantasy

Angel Rising Book 1

Angel Rising also on audio

Angel Hunter Book 2

Angel Guardian Book 2.5

Lost Gods

A romantic fantasy

Zeus Book 1

Ledo Book 2

Linc Book 3

CHILDREN OF THE WAVES

A romantic fantasy

Sea Bride

Sea Storm

Sea Witch

Sea Child

The Children of the Waves Collection Books 1-3 in KU

CROXROADS

An action adventure urban fantasy

Wild Child

Wild Fire

Wild Magic

CroXroads Box Set

THE ELEMENTALS

A medieval fantasy

Journey of the Princess of Ice- A graphic Novella Edition

The Beast Within World

A paranormal fantasy romance

The Beast Within

Audible also Coming Soon-

The Hidden Series

A dark paranormal romance

Dark Mist

Dark Shadow

WRITING AS URSULA SINCLAIR

FANTASY/PARANORMAL/SCI/FI/NEW ADULT

The City of Sin
>   After Midnight- City of Sin
>   When Dawn Comes- City of Sin
>   The Eventide Hour- City of Sin

Contemporary
>   *The Ballerina Series*
>   Contemporary new adult

The Ballerina & The Fighter- Book 1
>   Maze- The Ballerina Series Book 2
>   The Dancer- The Ballerina Series Book 3
>   The Ballerina Series Collection- Books 1-3

Young Guns
>   Contemporary new adult
>   The Prison Guard's Son- Young Guns Book 1

The Martini Lounge
>   Contemporary new adult (can be read as stand alones)

Shaken- The Martini Lounge (also Young Guns Book 1.5)
Stirred- The Martini Lounge
Frozen- The Martini Lounge

The Guardian Agency
Romantic suspense

White Wedding- The Guardian Agency Series Book 1
Something Blue- The Guardian Agency Series Book 2
Wine and Roses- The Guardian Agency Series Book 3
Guardian Agents Boxed Set

Sci/fi
Shadow Wars
Sci/fi new adult

Shadow Wars Homebound

Co-Written

The Maji Series co-written with Phoenix Daniels
A paranormal romance

The Cigar King in KU

Defiant co-written with Kassanna writing as Ursula Sinclair
A new adult contemporary romance

STAND ALONES

The Princess Bed
A fairytale fantasy romance

The Glass King
A fantasy romance

The Christmas Spirit
A holiday romantic fantasy short

Day in the Sun
A futuristic sc/fi romance

Come To Me
A contemporary romance
Hold On
Contemporary romantic suspense

FREE ON PROLIFIC WITH SIGN UP

Tears On A Rose
    Tatianna

Coming 2020/2021
    Soul Collectors full length
    Quiet Strength
    Wild Child- CroXroads full length (June 6th Pre-order Now)
    Chances Are
    Dark Soul- The Hidden Series Book 3
    Sea Child- Children of the Waves Book 4
    Choose Me- The Ballerina Series Book 4
    The Otherworlders- Wolfen (Ursula Sinclair)- New Adult
    Shadow Wars Ronin Riders (Ursula Sinclair)- New Adult
    Living On The Edge- The Clan
    Skye High
    Promises
    Kissed By A Rose
    Lexi's Journal
    The Ice Man Cometh- The Elementals Book 2

OTHER BOOKS BY KASSANNA

Pack Rulez

(Volkshire Pack, Betaille Coalition, Rattler, Texas Clutch. Feria Train
and Black Mountain Pack)

Scar

Kuma

Fangs

Claws

Hiss

Pack

Misère

Omega

Roar

Noir

Redemption

Pride Riders

(Lyons Motorcycle Club)

Prey

Primal

Prowl

Shifter Legends

(Beasts that have been around a Millennia- Ancient Ones who only
exist in Legends...)

Rogue Dragon

Stone Guardian

Defiant Dragon

Beast Protector